THE DISTANCE MEASURED IN DAYS

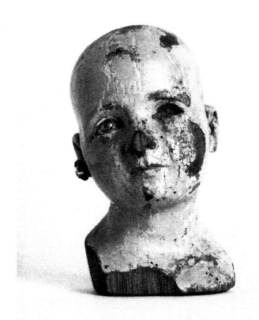

Anthony Howell

The Distance Measured in Days

A NOVEL

Grey Suit Editions

First published in 2021 by
Grey Suit Editions, an affiliate
of Phoenix Publishing House Ltd

British Library Cataloguing in Publication Data
A C.I.P. catalogue record for this book is available
from the British Library

Paperback ISBN: 978-1-903006-19-1
e-book ISBN: 978-1-903006-20-7

Designed and typeset in Monotype Bembo by Anvil

Printed and bound in the United Kingdom
by Hobbs the Printers Ltd

Grey Suit Editions
33 Holcombe Road, London N17 9AS
https://greysuiteditions.co.uk/

for Signe

Contents

Chapter 1	11
Chapter 2	28
Chapter 3	47
Chapter 4	65
Chapter 5	82
Chapter 6	101
Chapter 7	119
Chapter 8	138
Chapter 9	156
Chapter 10	174
Chapter 11	191
Chapter 12	209
Chapter 13	228

The Distance Measured
in Days

I

WE HIRE camels and a guide, and later in the day we ride out of the village. Our camels dip and lurch along on their flat, cloven pads. Slowly we approach a sign – *Timbuctoo; 40 jours*. We come abreast of it, and then we plod past it. Our guide leads us across a dry plain. We pass a broken house, and further on the skull of an ass. Otherwise there is nothing. Now we begin to ache. Soon our thighs are chafed. The motion is faintly sickening, and the soft-footed beasts travel forward at such a tedious pace that the arid landscape appears never to shift. By dusk however we find ourselves among some low hills of sandy shale which slope away from a few stunted bushes. The guide orders his camel to kneel. We imitate his order as best we can, and our camels sink, forefeet first, settling on the ground. This descent is worse than the journey. We are thrown forwards and then back in our saddles. Inge gasps. The camels grunt as they become one with the desert.

Stiffly Inge and I dismount. Within minutes several tribesmen have materialised out of nowhere. Men speak quietly as evening cools the day. A tent goes up. Water comes from a jerry-can our guide carries with him. The sun sinks, leaving a glow in the west. Now the guide pummels flour and water into dough. He places the flattened, circular shape he has made on a low bed of embers. Then he covers the dough and the embers with sand.

A thin smoke rises in the twilight.

HER BREATH came in gasps. She was thrown forwards and then back. That was what it sounded like. The room was very dark. Meanwhile Harry lay on top of Rachel. Rachel lay on a duvet spread over the kelims on the bedroom floor. Inge and Rodney were going at it on the bed. Taking his weight on his elbows, Harry kept quite still on Rachel's hips. On each of his thrusts into her, Rodney seemed to knock the breath out of Inge's body. Steve was there in the bedroom as well, and Ingrid. You could see nobody. They had all serviced each other's partners. Steve and Ingrid were somewhere on the floor, on a mattress. Harry could feel the rough weave of a kelim under his knee. He was happy to listen to Inge. Her expelled breath was evidence that nobody felt possessive, nobody thought they owned anyone else. He had just come inside Rachel. That had been quite an effort since he had come inside Ingrid less than half-an-hour earlier. It was a shame really. Ingrid's skin was coarse. She had moved beneath him in a rather sluggish way. He had not met her before that night. She was somebody's *au pair*, and she had been asked over merely as a partner for Steve. Rachel was different. She was pretty and slim, white of skin and intelligent. He and Inge had met her in Turkey at the same time as they had met Rodney. She was Rodney's constant companion, and Harry had always fancied her. Now, when the opportunity arose, it had proved more of an effort than a pleasure. Still, from the way she was gasping, Inge seemed to be enjoying herself.

Harry dwelt on that night, as he dwelt on the night when Inge had slept with Charlie and Jane. This he had only been told about by Inge. Nevertheless he dwelt upon it. He was keen to have Inge with another woman, just as Charlie had done.

To witness the manifestation of your friend's appetite was a singular proof of love. There was an honesty about it. If their appetite was for someone other than you that was alright. It was your hang-up if you couldn't take it.

Such liberated notions were Harry's gospel, and Inge went along with his ideas. She was a fine-looking girl. There were tall men who desired to give her pleasure. Harry was not so tall, but Inge still respected him, and she enjoyed his body. Together they embarked on adventures and tasted many nights of experiment.

AFTER THE BIRTH of their daughter Dawn, these nights of experiment were curtailed. Inge had her studies, and when she was not studying she was looking after the baby. She seemed to resent him talking about other girls or wishing to continue their experiments. Harry dwelt on her gasping under Rodney. He dwelt on her lying there between Jane and Charlie. Before Dawn was a year old, he had walked out on Inge. Perhaps it was only a gesture. Even so, he began having an affair with a free-and-easy girl whose name was Rosemary. He was living in a friend's flat in Belsize Park while the friend visited New York. And so it seemed that they had split up. But walking out was probably only a gesture on Harry's part. Pretty soon his friend would have arrived back from New York. Harry would never have started to pay rent when he could live in the house with Inge. He was not terribly serious about Rosemary either. He was serious about being free to have an affair though. But he did need to see Dawn. Dawn was his daughter after all. One afternoon, after having left Inge, he had condescended to visit the house.

AND SO WE had driven to Kew. We parked Inge's car and went in through the gates. It was winter. On the grass under a black tree I squatted down on my haunches. Somehow this meant freedom. We could split up for good now. Not just as a gesture. It could mean complete freedom to be myself again, and for as long as I wanted – not just for a few bachelor days in a friend's absented flat. Even in the cold, I then began to feel hot. How could I think this thought? Shouldn't we immediately have another? Surely I had to offer that?

Inge had walked on through the bleak gardens. Now, slowly, she returned to where I squatted under the black tree. My hands were pushed into my pockets. I had not seen our daughter dead and blue. Inge had told me of this. She had turned blue. I had not seen her myself. I had not pushed through the double-doors to look. After Inge's call, I had hurried over to the hospital in a taxi. Inge had met me outside. 'Don't go in,' she had said. 'It's too late. You don't need to see her.' She had said it only to spare me the sight. But then my nerve had failed. I had simply nodded my head. I had not insisted. Did I want to see her dead and blue? My daughter? Well, I agreed to leave it, to leave her there unseen, behind the double-doors. We had gone home from the hospital in the taxi.

She thinks it makes him surly – which it does. Still, he insists on smoking.

Smoking is one of his pleasures. His other pleasure is sex. He finds both irresistible. On its own, neither one of these hankerings demands much of an outlay. In combination though, they call for a large one.

Each of these cravings affects the other. Often, when he gets stoned, he turns into a remote creature, not at all interested in sex. At other times he is only excited by making love and not very keen on getting high. There have been occasions when he has got stoned and then made love, but then the love-making has seldom proved satisfactory. On certain rare occasions, he has recognised that sex can be a problem. But it has hardly ever occurred to him that dope can be one too.

He was first offered some grass among the dunes near Cap Ferret. At the time he had been reading English at university and was a member of the university's gymnastics team. The team was coming back from an inter-varsity event in Madrid. They were travelling in a minibus and stopping at campsites each night.

They went around in shorts and track-suits. Harry had gained the highest number of points for his exercises on the mat, but his team had been knocked out of the tournament. It had been a time of frustration. Some very fey young men had hung around the team, often offering to take its members to dinner and then afterwards attempting to seduce them. This had annoyed Harry. It was not just that the young men fancied him – that he could take in his stride. It was their effete manner which had offended him. They had all been frightful queens. Alright, a man might like a man, but why should he act like a woman to prove it – and not even like a woman – like some caricature of one? Yet some of his team-mates went along with this nonsense. Harry felt under pressure. Their antics got his goat. Such behaviour had nothing to do with his sport, and nothing to do with the discipline that was required of it.

Yet at the same time he was often irritated by their coach, who insisted that talent was merely a matter of discipline and sometimes set them useless and convoluted exercises justified solely by his wish to teach them obedience. Harry had begun to question this dogma. It seemed to lead only to regimental results. From a very early age, Harry had been an exceptional gymnast, but now, as he went through university, he was looking more towards poetry, which he had always written. Gymnastics was beginning to seem limited.

A young American who had been in Viet-Nam occupied a tent near to that of the team. Like them, he was only passing through; but he and Harry happened to strike up a conversation by the wash-basins. Then the American offered Harry a joint.

Night had just fallen, and the moon was full. The American took him behind a dune and they turned on. The American told Harry to hold the smoke in for as long as he possibly could. He patted Harry on the shoulder and went away.

Harry strolled among the dunes, with the turpentine pines of that region on one side of him and the sea on the other. The large moon was shimmering on the waves. He ran down the side of a dune, and his run seemed to last forever. The ocean leapt, and each wave was distinct. The sand stretched into timelessness. It was flat, but it rippled beneath his feet, and its ripples were like the hardened sides of thousands of small fishes. The sea shimmered, and glittered and glimmered, as if it were all silver. He ran and turned an Arab-spring, then leapt back and upwards into the air. Springing backwards, up and over he went, with a flick-flack under the moonlight. It was indescribable. Everything enlarged. He tried dope again, and sometimes it was good. Once, in summer, he saw every drop of spray sprinkling from a hose, every crumb of pollen on the petals. He walked barefoot over the lawn and could feel the hairs on the grass-blades.

But dope has less effect the more he uses it. And the less effect it has, the more he uses the stuff.

When he gets stoned, he loses his temper, or at least he may lose his temper if the conditions for smoking are not absolutely right. The right music, the right surroundings, the right company. Once he got stoned and watched a friend's baby focusing on a cuddly elephant, and separating its image from the settee on which it rested. It was magical to watch the baby's mind at work. There was nothing juvenile about that pre-verbal intelligence, rather there was something ancient about the baby's wisdom. Perhaps it had to do with its baldness, the chubby folds of the torso. There was some quality the infant shared with Buddha. Harry was fascinated by this.

Since Dawn has arrived though, conditions never seem

right for smoking. He rolls up his grass and puts on a record, and then his daughter starts to cry. After her birth, he never finds himself looking at the moonlight. More often than not he finds himself staring with dope-glazed eyes at a bundle of shit-smeared nappies. Inge is right when she says it makes him surly.

Rosemary has dope. She offers some to Harry at a party. She's been going out with Dick, and this is Dick's party. But Rosemary is as free as can be. She has brought some of her own friends along, she has brought dope, and she'll get Harry stoned.

Harry is talking to Laura, a large lady in a smock of Indian muslin whose hair is piled untidily on her head. Dick's place is packed, mainly with poets and publishers. Everyone is crowded around the bottles, dips and celery sticks in the kitchen.

'Where's Inge?' Laura asks.

'Studying, of course. Inge does nothing but study these days. It's very dull for me.'

'Dullness is what marriage is about, Harry. I should know. I've done it twice.'

'But why should it be dull? Nothing's changed. Inge's got her figure back. I still fancy her. She was sewn up marvellously tight. Why should, it be dull? I don't see why we have to stop having adventures.'

'That's the way it goes, Harry. That's the way it goes.'

Just then Rosemary comes up with a joint in her hand. She puts the joint in Harry's mouth, and while he inhales she feels him through his trousers. Laura moves away.

Harry has promised not to get stoned. Inge will be

furious. She's sure to find out. She can tell at a glance when he is. And if he arrives home late she will guess the reason.

Rosemary and her friends are going on somewhere else. She invites Harry to come along with them. This exasperates Dick. But Harry takes no notice. He leaves the party with Rosemary and her friends.

His subsequent night on the tiles marks the beginning of his bust-up with Inge. Perhaps it is only a gesture. But Inge hears all about it from Dick. She takes a dislike to Rosemary, more for Dick's sake than because of her fooling around with Harry.

Rosemary allows Harry to fondle her. It is she who instigates these proceedings. Harry is high as a kite. He feels he can be free with this girl. They go out onto the pavement, and he puts his hand on her bum. She pushes back nicely against him, and the door slams behind them. They get into a car . . .

ONE AFTERNOON, after having left Inge, I condescend to visit the house. Dawn is zipped into her pink romper-suit. Inge says little, but she puts on the kettle for tea while I play with my daughter. I sit on the steps which lead down from the dining-room (which is an extension of the kitchen) into the large reception room we have had made by knocking two smaller rooms into one. Dawn crawls towards me across the cork tiles. I pretend to be a tiger. I growl deep in my throat, and she gurgles with pleasure and crawls rapidly away under the dining-room table, pausing once to look back and grin at me. I crawl under the table after Dawn. Then I crawl away from her and she

crawls after me. It's funny how she does that. I smile.
Things are going to work out. But I rise to go.

'Aren't you going to stay now?' Inge asks.

'Not tonight.'

Nevertheless I sigh as I put on my overcoat. I don't
really want to go. This will be my last gesture, a final signal
of my claim to freedom. Things are going to work out.
Tomorrow night I'll be back, I think. I shrug at Inge and
leave.

HE ROLLED over and put his hand on her thigh. She curled
herself more tightly into a ball. Then he tugged her hip.

'Leave me alone.'

'Why should I?'

'Leave me alone. You're stoned.'

'But I like doing it when I'm stoned.'

'I don't like it. I can't bear it when you're stoned.'

He rolled away from her and made himself into a ball
as well, at the same time pulling the bedclothes off her.
She tugged them back in her own direction, and then he
yanked them his way, twice as hard.

It was not always like this. Sometimes they would play
a game in bed. Inge would lie on her back in the dark,
perfectly still, ostensibly asleep. Ever so lightly, Harry would
let his fingers brush her tummy. Then he would move his
hand in the dark and touch her ever so lightly under the
knee. Next he would pause, with his hand beneath the
sheet hovering over her skin. Then he would touch her
hip or brush her thigh. Inge would shake, and then again
lie still. Harry would try to do it so that it seemed as if his

touches were mere accidents. He would never allow his fingers to brush her twice in the same place. He was always trying to defeat her expectations of where she might be touched next. Sometimes his fingertip would make contact just at the plumpest part of her inner leg. Then he would brush her knee-cap or her waist. The touches were lighter than stroking; a hint at her loins, a hair's displacement. Inge would shiver and sigh. Then he would lightly prod her slit. The game would make her damp.

But none of this would work when he was stoned. Then it was better to stay dressed and write.

After Dawn was born, Harry got stoned a lot, and they left off playing the touching, brushing and prodding game. Most of the time in Morocco, and after they came back from Morocco, they rolled into separate balls and slept back to back. It was only in the desert that they clung to each other.

By the time Harry got to Manila he was feeling starved for love. Beautiful brown young girls looked after him. They were most of them students at the academy of cinema. They smiled and stroked his neck. But he was never alone with any one of them. They would seem perfectly charming and would dance with him on the roofs of hotels at receptions held for the delegates. Yet they never let him kiss them on the mouth. Harry accused them all of being flirts, but they laughed and shook their heads and said no, they were not flirts at all. They really liked him, but they had only been recruited to make the congress go with a swing. There were some beautiful brown young boys recruited as well as the girls.

That night we slept in the tent under a single blanket. The heat of the day had not prepared us for the chill of the night. Our guide and the tribesmen slept outside, close to the camp-fire. The desert floor was very hard. Inge and I kept all our clothes on. Without wishing for intimacy, we huddled together. I sensed that this was a test – another tough experience to share. It was so cold it was hard to get to sleep. I felt that only a thin layer of sand covered the solid rock beneath us. We lay against the hardness of the world, huddled together under a thin blanket. There had been a reason for coming. There had been a need to get away from clatter, mental clatter as well as the audible sort we had experienced in Marrakesh. While jolting over the mountains in the bus, the Sahara had seemed a goal. There had been a reason for coming out here, but now we huddled together in the middle of nowhere. Outside the tent, the tribesmen shifted closer to the dying fire. An occasional cough could be heard.

WITHIN AN HOUR, many of their friends are with them. It is not long after they have driven back from Kew. These are their real friends; the ones they never service. The ones with whom they talk about art and anthropology. They are too seriously involved with these people to make love to them. The people they service are throw-away people; people who give them pleasure. But these have never been their serious friends. Their serious friends are systemic musicians and conceptual artists, poets interested in abstraction and minimalist sculptors. Others are neurophysicists, neo-Keynesian economists and performance artists. Harry has started a magazine, and practically all of his friends are the co-editors.

A while back, there was a gathering. Harry talked about the idea of the text. Inge brought up the Trobriand Islanders. Harry maintained that language needed to emancipate itself from narrative. Narrative was to writing what figuration was to painting. Inge insisted that it was absurd to suppose that the islanders could see no connection between intercourse and birth. Theories like this told you more about the ethnographers who came up with such findings than they did about the islanders themselves.

'But I thought the poetic muse was originally associated with the memory,' said Myfanwy, who was a poet herself. 'How can you deal with the memory without narrative?'

'I couldn't care less about memory. Narrative forces us into the past. But the past has set like cement. I'm into the continuous present. I want to live in a state of flux. I suppose it's anarchy really. But if I'm an anarchist, then I want the writing to be anarchy as well.'

'When it comes to anarchy, you can't beat the police,' observed a friend called Robert.

'What do you mean by that?'

'I'm quoting Bernard Shaw.'

'Those ethnographers were positively Victorian,' said Inge. 'Well, they were Victorians. They had Victorian values of course, and these values got reflected in their findings.'

'Aren't we just the same?' put in Anita. 'Don't our findings reflect our values?'

'Yes,' said an artist called Yehudah. 'We discover free love, drug cultures and licensed schizophrenia. We observe dream-time and property sharing among the indigenous groups we study because those are the items we are interested in today in our own society.'

'Violent anarchy isn't freedom it's fascism,' Harry went on. 'I'm into the pure anarchy of pleasure. I'll find release for myself by following up my desires, however selfish that may appear to others. If more people felt free to pursue their pleasures then the world might begin to work.'

'But men's vanity,' said Inge. 'That's just as much of a constant as the incest taboo. In one tribe they make a tremendous fuss about the husband when the wife is pregnant – everyone gathering around as he lies agonizing in simulated labour, while his wife goes off quietly into the woods.'

'I don't mean work in the sense of physical sweat. But if we all followed pleasure then the world might work as a system. While you're concerned with your own enjoyment you're not likely to interfere with the enjoyment of others. We can't go on suppressing ourselves.'

At this gathering, Inge and Harry sat apart from each other, holding forth at separate ends of the room. They talked at the same time, each about their own subject. Nevertheless they could hear what each other said.

Harry was still in full flight. 'That's how we suppress other people. And that's what leads to a clogged valve. Eventually the machine breaks down. It can't run on suppression.'

'Yes, but a lot of good energy is built up by suppression,' Yehudah responded. 'Sublimation of a desire can lead to some marvellous art. Suppression sets up a sort of fermentation process, I guess.'

Harry shook his head.

'I don't see it that way. Suppression makes everything tense. It's like that body-building method they call dynamic tension. You can lock your arms together and pit one muscle against another without letting the energy escape from your own body. That way you can build big muscles. They look good, but there's no suppleness to them.'

'That's what makes the job of the anthropologist so difficult. We see everything from our own standpoint. The Victorians look through Victorian eyes. And the man in that tribe sees birth entirely from a man's point of view.'

'They tear easily, those tension muscles. You can't use them on anything outside a gym because they haven't been developed through use. They're pumped up with pressure. I think that's the wrong way to build muscle. If you want strong, lean biceps it's better to go to the woods with an axe.'

Harry has always written poetry but since he has also been a gymnast his stomach muscles are still well defined. When in training, he had worked hard and disciplined his actions. He could do flick-flacks and turn double somersaults in the air. He had represented his university at the sport and took it very seriously indeed.

Then he began talking with friends who read philosophy. Blake and De Sade were often mentioned. He studied Provo literature and was impressed by the free white bicycles of Amsterdam. So he became a questioner. He began to see discipline as a strait-jacket. Eventually he gave up all forms of gymnastics except sexual gymnastics and those of the dance-floor. Now he has discovered anarchy in nature, and he equates the poetic imagination with riotous vegetation. But he does want his anarchy to work. He is forever looking for a system which promotes openness. Suppleness has become a symbolic quality. He thinks that there might be a more flexible way of organising society than that ordained by government.

In a somewhat theatrical context, it is just this sort of workable anarchy that he comes across in the square outside the Marrakesh bazaar. Here there is no single point of focus. Everyone is free to perform as they wish wherever they wish. The crowds drift from act to act. In one space, a man is allowing a snake to bite him on the forearm. In another, a troupe of tumblers are climbing up each other to form a human tree. In a far corner sits a pair of camels. Next to them, a mechanic is working beneath a car. It reminds Harry of a fair by Brueghel. Inge tugs his arm. A large crowd is gathering over to their right. They edge in among the other spectators, pushing closer and closer, until they can see. At first what is going on in the centre of this crowd does not appear to be very much at all. A brown gypsy woman wearing a red bandanna is squatting near a low fire.

THE WING DIPPED over islands, bays and lagoons; all partially hidden by shreds of cloud. I leaned forward to peer down through the porthole. The plane slid over palm trees onto the runway. It braked hard, and then taxied over the tarmac to roll to a stop in front of the main building. Moveable stairs were driven up against the hull. I was wearing my smartest suit, and I stepped out onto the metal platform at the top of the stairs. From that moment, I began to sweat. The heavy heat of the tropics enveloping me under the dull sky was unlike any heat I had ever known. And then, at the foot of the stairs, I could see that I was expected to negotiate a corridor of smiling brown girls dressed in brightly coloured sarongs. Around their necks hung garlands of cream-coloured, sweet-smelling flowers: I learnt to call them "frangipani". As I stepped down onto the tarmac I was embraced from all sides.

'Welcome! Welcome!'

Garlands were thrown over my head. My cheeks were touched by soft, laughing lips. Everywhere the scent of frangipani.

2

I T'S AS THOUGH she had suffocated. But why? Very little is known about it. A certain percentage of babies just happen to die suddenly each year. Various theories have been put forward. Some babies may have allergies to powdered milk. Or they may react badly to sudden changes in room temperature. No virus has been identified. The cause remains mysterious, though heredity may affect the syndrome. The child turns blue, just as if someone had thrust a pillow over its face. Why do these small beings retire from life so early? Perhaps they die of loneliness or fright. In romantic novels you can die of a broken heart, so perhaps a baby can die of a broken heart. In ghost stories you can die of fright, so perhaps a baby can die of fright. The jagged gash of lightning. The crack of thunder coming immediately upon it. And the whole house gets a shake. Animals can die of grief or terror. Their breath comes in gasps. I remember a tiny pink mouth opening and then shutting, and no air going in or coming out. Then it is over. I sit with the small, furry corpse cradled in my hands.

SO NOW INGE stands near him where he squats by the black tree at Kew. A while before, the taxi brought them home from the hospital, but as they got to the front door Inge said, 'I can't go in.'

'Have you got your car-keys?' he asked quietly.

'Yes, in my bag. But that's in the house.'

He paid the taxi, and it drove away. While Inge waited on the pavement, he let himself in with his key. Her bag was on the table in the dining-room. Without looking at anything else, he walked out of the house and shut the door behind him. He handed Inge her bag.

'Let's go for a drive.'

And so they have driven to Kew. It is a few weeks after Christmas, on a chill day. There are no leaves on the trees. He has squatted down, and Inge has walked away. He has been staring at the grass between his feet. And at length, walking slowly, Inge has come back to him. Harry remains in a squat with his hands pushed in his pockets. He can feel Inge standing near him, but he can't bring himself to look at her.

'Oh, God, what have I done?' she says.

Harry stays close to the ground, like a man who has been punched in the stomach.

'I think she was crying earlier. Anyhow, I just let her cry. I was so tired and fed up, you know.'

'I know.'

'And then, when I went in to her, it must have been about nine, she was lying like that, all blue. I tried everything. I tried slapping her. I tried giving her the kiss of life. There was only this awful rasp in her lungs, every so often. I think I was just too late. I got Delphina to ring the hospital. And the ambulance came straight away. They tried to do what they could. But they said there was just nothing they could do. And all the time she just lay there, going more and more blue and clenched up, with a terrible little grimace on her face. It must have been so hard on her.'

'I know, Inge.' His eyes sting. Inge bites her lip.

THERE WERE MEN with snakes, and acrobats, and many men with drums. One man was allowing his snake to bite his forearm. Inge and Harry had come into the hard sunlight of the main square after wandering up a narrow street where rugs were sold. They had looked in a desultory way at the rugs. Bitten by one's own snake. Harry repeated the phrase to himself later, after they had checked out of their hotel. They had boarded a bus and were rattling over the mountains towards the Sahara. Bitten by one's own snake. Maybe he could get a poem out of that. But then there was too much meaning in the phrase. Inge stared out of the window through a film of dust as they came slowly down from the pass. Harry glanced at her and then turned to face forwards again. It was no good returning to symbols. He was interested in words as words – as realities rather than signifiers. But not that concrete stuff. Had to be some minimal change, enough to constitute thought – which was why permutations – one's own bitten snake by – but how get beyond permutations? Snake bitten by one's own. By one's own bitten snake. But systems got in the way. Too constricting. Writing them out without error required such discipline that discipline appeared their only merit. A mental moo for discipline. Had to be done with that. Wanted something less pre-ordained. And now he caught himself not thinking about Dawn. Only a week since the day they had driven to Kew and already back into his own trip. Nothing as urgent as the quest. As the quest as urgent nothing. Quest for abstract poetry. Do in words what Glass had done in sound. Yes, but too predictable. Rule-bound. For Harry felt a need to release himself from his rules, and in the future free to feel some other need. Yeats's father had said that a poet was free to change his mind once a fortnight. Freedom from rules was the trip for a change, while rules might be the change of trip tomorrow. But what never changed was the freedom to choose his own trip. People said that about him. Inge said he never saw anything from her point of view. But how could you see something from anyone else's point of view? You were inside yourself, not inside someone else. Your world was the only world you saw. Bitten by your own snake.

They rolled to a stop. He and Inge stepped down from the bus with their bags. They stood in the centre of a wide, sloping square. It was wide and white, so wide that the white, flat-roofed houses looked small at its edge. There was no one around, other than the few who had also stepped off the bus. These were all local people, and they walked rapidly away with their trussed chickens and their rolled blankets. The driver went to the back of his bus and lay down. The engine of the bus ticked, otherwise there was silence. Above, the sky was large and blue. This was the last village before the desert. You could get no further by car or by truck.

From a very long distance away, a small blur of deeper blue approached. This blur enlarged until it became a billowing robe; the attire of a handsome, dark young man.

'Salaam Aleikoom, voulez-vous l'hôtel?'

'Nous voulons voyager dans le désert sur des chameaux.'

'Ça je peux arranger pour vous. Quand est-ce que vous voulez partir?'

'Est-ce que c'est possible de partir aujourd'hui?'

'Je peux arranger ça pour demain. Il faut que vous louer les chameaux et un guide. Mais maintenant je vais vous montre l'hôtel.'

They booked into the hotel and were shown to a bare room with a low bed and a small wash-basin. Grains of sand lay sprinkled on the tiled floor. They went out, intending to spend the rest of the day exploring the village. It turned out that there was very little to explore – only the wide square and the beginnings of a single street. Beyond that there was a plain covered with small white stones, then a series of low hills. There was one café, where they sat until dark, each reading a book. Then they ate kebabs with bread. After that they returned to their hotel and went straight to bed, where they slept, back against back.

But the next day they rode into the desert, over the plain covered with the small white stones. Before nightfall their camels knelt. A fire was lit, and a tent was pitched. During the ride, Inge had tried to keep abreast of Harry, in order that they might exchange observations about their experience. She managed this a few times, but her camel seemed to prefer to follow in Harry's wake, and its strange gait felt so irregular that really all she could do was hang on. Harry tried to rein back. But the camels were obviously accustomed to walking in single file.

Their first night in the desert was a shock. Harry had insisted that they bring jumpers, despite the heat of the day. Yet the night was even colder than he had anticipated.

Once the sun went down, all the heat drained from the ground. There was nothing there to retain the heat. They were not in the least prepared for the intensity of the cold. And so they had shivered while they slept. The dawn came, and the sun rose, but the heat returned more slowly than the light. They stamped their feet and swung their arms. Both felt terribly stiff. But there was no turning back. Before the sun had risen far into the sky they had mounted their camels and set out again across the waste.

I HAD WOKEN before the dawn. It was still bitterly cold. Inge remained clenched up, stunned into sleep by exhaustion at last, under the threadbare blanket. A pallid light began to penetrate the canvas. I crawled out of the tent. Darkness stretched endlessly away from me in all directions, with only a faint suggestion of light diminishing that darkness in the sky. Nothing yet distinguished the desert. I shivered and shivered again. Very, very dimly, I could make out mounds like graves at my feet where the guide and several tribesmen lay asleep around the cold embers of their fire. I walked swiftly away from the camp and nearly fell over the camels. These larger objects slept where they knelt in their hobbles.

A crimson line appeared in the east. Gradually a skyline became evident. Beyond, the camels I could make out the silhouette of a single stunted bush. Light began to return to the world. Beyond the bush there was nothing. A brown haze of nothingness and nothing else. I returned to the camp. Our guide was standing on his feet. He grunted a word of greeting. Soon the fire was restarted. Water was boiled. Inge came crawling out of the tent. She stretched awkwardly. Then she swung her arms. Her face looked drained and pinched. Small cups of black tea were put into our hands. The sun appeared. A few palm trees could now be seen, stones and more bushes. The sand and the rock took on colours.

'It's so still,' said Inge.

The guide beckoned. While we stood by him watching he knelt down and cleared away the sand. Out of the desert he lifted the loaf he had buried. Swiftly he brushed off the sand. Then he broke the bread and handed a piece to me and a piece to Inge. Under its crust, the white flesh of the loaf was warm. It was the best bread we had ever tasted.

DICK GETS INTO a huff of course, but Rosemary is quite prepared to try another sample. Later she lies beside Harry, gently frigging his limp penis after he has come inside her.

'They've told me I can't have one,' she explains. 'I've had two miscarriages, and then I got this infection last year – it's alright now, but they say that it's affected my ovaries. But I don't reckon I'm infertile. I reckon it depends on the sperm. If I find the right sperm I'll conceive again. I know I will. So I've had just about everybody I've met recently.'

Harry begins to go hard again. He strokes Rosemary's flanks.

'Have you ever done it with more than one person?'

'I don't mind how I do it, or who's there, so long as I end up with sperm inside me.'

Rosemary's skin feels dry. Her body is hot to the touch.

'What makes you so keen on having it with two people?'

'Well, I guess it turns me on. The trouble about being married is you feel totally approved of. All the relatives at the wedding, you know, sipping champagne and approving of two of you. When you were living together it was different. That was an illicit thing to do. But you see, I really like that. Feeling that they don't approve. Being a naughty boy.'

Rosemary gets astride his hips. She lowers herself onto his penis. Then she begins grinding her bottom against the tops of his thighs.

'It's not just that it's naughty though,' he goes on, looking directly into her eyes. 'Being with more than one person gets one away from that couples-in-love sort of crap. You know, like every ad on the box is about.'

Harry feels that he's putting it across in her own terms – after all, she's not an intellectual, indeed she seems less interested in his discourse than in rubbing his nipples into points. Nevertheless, he perseveres.

'Love reminds me of Andrex. Images of people terribly in love say Hotpoint to me or Zanussi. Being terribly in love is just a commodity-enhancing media conspiracy. I find it an absolute turn-off. People who really get on prefer observing each other's desires. It's about being rude with friends.'

Rosemary bends forwards and brushes his face with her dry lips. She nips his neck, and her breasts dangle against his chest. He lifts his hips towards her.

'How would you like to be rude with me?' she whispers.

'I'd like to have you with Inge. I'd like to have her kiss your lips while I put my fingers in both of you.'

'That would be lovely. Go on.'

Harry goes on, in more and more detail, until he comes inside her again. Rosemary slumps over him and soon falls asleep. The candle at the bedside is still burning. Without waking her up, he slides from beneath her. The room is a mess of cheap materials and empty wine-bottles caked with the drippings from previous candles. He sits on the side of the bed and rolls himself a single-paper joint of her grass. This he lights from the candle and inhales.

The best times with Inge have been far better than this. Rosemary is hot and dry. Only his spit makes her at all slippery — spit, and his previous sperm. Her nipples appear to harden, but he guesses that they are always hard. Slowly he exhales. The bases of the bottles gleam in shaken candle flame. He picks up a twinkling piece of costume jewellery. There are several Tantric posters on the walls. Cheap Tantric posters. Inge would sniff at these.

Inge is uptight now, but she has not always been so uptight. They have shared Steve, and that was lovely. And when they have been alone, Inge has sometimes been playful. Harry has even got her to dress up in his string vest, as well as to wear stockings and suspenders. Among artists and writers, these enticements seem all the more scandalous because of their trite vulgarity, yet for Harry's sake Inge has been prepared to go along with these clichés of desire, while he's been prepared to do as she wishes, if he can guess what she wants. Inge prefers him to guess her needs – she doesn't like to spell them out – and sometimes he succeeds. Sometimes he can make her more wet than any woman he has ever gone with.

It was like that the summer before last. They had gone on a holiday to Norway. Inge told him about midsummer night disease. This is when the men queue up at the doctor's the next morning with their pricks stuck in their zips. Inge and Harry laughed a lot that summer. She was keen to flirt with the potter and his wife. Then it was Harry who had held back. Inge felt so ripe. She was not on the pill, and she looked so beautiful, and she seemed so confident in her own country. Love-making was uppermost in their minds. They had made themselves a secret nest in the heather above the fiord.

THE NIGHT AFTER my visit to our house we meet at a party. Actually to say that we meet is a bit of an exaggeration. Dawn is there in her blue romper-suit, clinging to Inge's shoulder. I've come to the party with Rosemary. Inge ignores me. At this point in time, I'm completely obsessed by Rosemary. Rosemary seems on fire. She is naked beneath her woollen dress. When I feel her I can tell that she's wearing nothing underneath. I first met her at Dick's party. At the time, she was screwing Dick. But then she was screwing everybody, even her landlord. The night before she met Dick, she had invited the cab-driver to come upstairs with her after she'd paid her fare. Rosemary really does want a sample of everybody's sperm. She feels sure that some sperm will work for her where other sperm has not. The right sperm will get her what she wants. I'm turned-on by her availability. I'm violently attracted to her because she doesn't care what people think. I guess she's the epitome of freedom. I've stolen her off Dick in so far as it is possible to steal anyone so readily available. Dick is in a huff of course, but Rosemary is quite prepared to try another sample.

'WE CALL IT the ghetto,' his friend replied. Their chauffeur-driven car cruised on past the white wall of thirty-foot-high boards behind which little could be seen.

Harry turned to the palm-fringed, glittering sea. It was unbelievable to be here, thousands of miles away suddenly. Thousands of miles from Inge.

'You're not going to go, are you?' she had asked, when he had shown her the telegram he had found waiting for him on their return from Morocco.

He had moved away from her and stared out through the window at the grey street.

'Well, Inge, I'll never get another chance.'

'Don't go.'

'Basically, I ought to. It's very good for my career, you know. I don't think I should get a reputation for turning down this sort of thing.'

'Harry, how can you? Oh, please don't. I can't bear to be alone here. Not for a while.'

He had sat down on the sofa with his hands deep in his pockets.

'Very well, then. I won't, I suppose. I'll have to put them off.'

She had sat down next to him and had taken his arm.

'I'm so pleased, Harry. I don't want you to go.'

Then there had been a silence.

The chauffeur-driven car glided smoothly on, and Miranda Cruz was babbling something in his ear. Large hotels slid past them. Palms waved in the breeze. Harry remembered how odd it had felt back in their house. The cot had gone, and the baby-cage had been stored away. Dawn's romper-suits and little shirts had all been packed into bags and shoved out of sight. They could be given to someone else with a baby.

There was no evidence that Dawn had ever been there. Nevertheless their house was haunted by her small ghost. When he looked at the dining-room table he recalled crawling beneath it, pretending to be a tiger. She had just learnt to climb the stairs. And now she was a small ghost wailing quietly for exorcism. Inge would not go into the little bedroom which had been Dawn's bedroom, although it would have made her an excellent study. The feeling of absence kept recreating her presence. It had been like this after her funeral. They had not wanted to stay there then. It was little better now.

After the funeral, his mother had suggested that they get away. The funeral itself had been a trial. Harry had found it difficult to express any sadness. Mostly he felt bewildered, and from her external actions it seemed that Inge felt much the same. They were both trying to cope. His mother however was quite given over to grief. She was a breeder of dogs and horses, and she related to foals and pups more easily than she did to human beings. With humans she behaved stiltedly and was often at a loss for words. Children were a different matter. The smaller the human, the more of an animal it seemed to her. Her love of Dawn had been absolute, and her pride at being a grandmother had been considerable. She had aged visibly since Dawn had died. She had slowed down. She would sit on their sofa for a long time without saying anything, and then suddenly remind them of some small action of her grand-daughter's. This great sadness obstructed the sadness Harry sought to express.

'You must have another child,' she kept saying. 'You must have another child, you know. It's the only thing to do.'

But the house remained Dawn's territory. The stairs up to the first floor were the stairs she had learnt to negotiate, and the dining-room was where she had fled on all fours, turning only to grin at the tiger who was after her. Inge and Harry both felt bewildered. They needed to get away.

So after the funeral his mother paid for them to fly off to Morocco.

I SAT DOWN at the table and began to roll a joint. I was using some very good grass, so there was no call for tobacco. Crumbling lumps of warmed-up hashish onto tobacco is the usual British way of making a joint. I've always preferred the American way: a joint of grass, and nothing but grass, rolled in a single paper.

Not long before, I had taken up the offer of a residency on an American campus. Inge was already pregnant. But leaving her to grow larger as she did up our house with her ex-husband, I took wing for the Mid-West. On arrival I was given a cheque-book and an apartment. This enabled me to concentrate on my writing and to smoke some wonderful grass. During my time there, I serviced a succession of girls who were majoring in poetry as well as the very pretty wife of a local dentist. Inge joined me in New York for Christmas and then flew back to enlarge still more in London. Her ex-husband was a painter, and he painted our house in imaginative colours. I flew back to the Mid-West. I completed a systemic text on the joys of making love and then flew to London. Our house was finished. It looked smart and exotic – a wonderful showcase for our kelims. Dawn was born a few months after my return.

Now we were spending a few wintry days at my mother's. I sat in our bedroom, lit up and inhaled while gazing rather languidly out of the window at the yard. The sky was dull to the point of whiteness, and the leafless trees on the heath beyond the yard were buffeted by gusts of violent wind. I had only recently taken up with Rosemary. I remembered the Mid-West with some regret and was at the time in the grip of an exasperated reaction to all things domestic. Baby matters disgusted me. I wanted to make love in a liberated way again. It was what I stood, for. I inhaled again. Inge came hurrying out of the house, pushing Dawn in her pram. She propelled the vehicle towards the front gate and then down the lane, and was soon out of sight, gone beyond the thicket of brambles and elders which had grown up around the compost heap. From

Inge's hasty movements, I guessed that she was furious. She obviously knew that I was smoking. She always knew, even when there was no evidence that I had smoked. Since having Dawn, Inge had gone off smoking. She hated me to smoke. She thought it made me surly – which it did.

THEY ARE BOTH proud of their kelims, which they have collected together on trips to Kayseri, Damascus and Tabriz. Purchasing kelims has taught them how to haggle.

'Two hundred? Far, far too much. I wouldn't give you fifty!'

Such remarks are usually expressed in body-language and signs. There is much lifting of chins, shoulder-shrugging and dismissive movements of the hands. It is very important to stride firmly away from the shop with one's nose in the air, and then to be seen sipping tea with another merchant in the bazaar.'

Inge is very good at all this. She is tall, and she possesses a brand of Scandinavian arrogance which proves devastating among the small brown men of these Middle-Eastern markets. Knowing just how to haggle is indicative of their experience of the Orient.

Their house back in London is full of kelims; a few of them spoilt by garish modern dyes. These are the first they purchased. Others have been slashed with knives, which shows that they have been used to cover the bodies of the dead – these are always good bargains.

Their best kelims are not laid on the floor. They are hung on the walls and treated with more respect than the paintings they have wheedled out of their artist friends.

The woven lozenges of these kelims are much admired by visitors. Then there are other kelims draped over chairs and over the sofa.

Harry's mother is very much a country person, Inge sometimes resents her visits. She arrives with muddy shoes which she always neglects to wipe on the doormat. Well may Inge wonder what she thinks the doormat is for. When she sits down on the sofa, she transfers her dog hairs to the kelims. Harry maintains that his mother owns far too many dogs. She has always had two of her own, and of course she inherited two from his grandmother when she died. Neither of the two lines – his grandmother's Dandie-Dinmonts, his mother's Afghan hounds – have subsequently been allowed to die out. As one bitch grows old, another bitch will have pups, and Harry's mother will keep one of the pups from a litter whenever a bitch grows senile. There are always far too many dogs around.

Harry is very critical of his mother, but at the same time he hotly resents Inge's criticisms of her muddy boots and her dog hairs. To attack her is to attack him in some way. Harry will retaliate by attacking Inge's parents. Inge's mother keeps their family home so clean that if she has spilt a splodge of mayonnaise on her gleaming Norwegian floorboards she can simply bend, scoop it up with a finger and pop the splodge in her mouth. This is a blatant tidiness which demonstrates how Inge's mother has nothing better to do than fuss around the house.

When Inge goes home to her parents she often finds the atmosphere quite stultifying. However, when she is in London, she sometimes feels that she respects their values.

It is as if she can only love them at a distance. Her irritation at Harry's taunts usually increases with the length of her absences from Norway.

Harry grew up on a farm. He has lived within the clumsy, untidy friendliness of animals. During his adolescence he reacted to his upbringing and embraced the slicker values of the town. Dog-shit on carpets annoys him, but otherwise his urban ways are something of a veneer. From an early age he has seen how animals are born. He has witnessed them being mated and has watched them as they died. He is used to wading through mud in fields. His childhood has been dirty and quirky. There are things he has known about which the other children in his class have not known about. But it has taken him a very long time to learn how to do up his laces, and no one at his mother's farm has ever told him to pull up his socks.

When Harry was eight years old, one of his mother's bitches went through a phantom pregnancy.

A SMALL WOMAN meets me at the end of the corridor of laughing faces. She places her own overpowering garland of frangipani around my neck and then kisses me on both cheeks.

'Welcome to the Philippines,' she cries.

Miranda Cruz and I became acquainted in the Mid-West. We were writers-in-residence at the same college. Miranda is a skinny, dark little woman. She reminds me of a monkey. Her legs are like sticks, and when she gets excited she waves her spider-monkey fingers at her listeners. She presides over part of the university in Manila, and it is through her good offices that I have been invited to the Afro-Asian Writers' Congress which is being hosted by Imelda Marcos. I am neither African nor Asian. My role is to be that of an observer-delegate. Now Miranda takes my arm. Next, I am waved through customs, still in my sweet-scented garlands. Miranda chatters incessantly. We get into a car.

I HAD WOKEN before the dawn. I had crawled out of the tent, shivering with cold. It was still very dark. I had walked past the vague mounds near the remains of the camp-fire, past the camels and away from the camp. Now I paused at a small, stunted bush which could barely be made out against the darkness of the desert and the mere glimmer of pallid light underscored by a crimson line to the east. I could walk on now, and get lost. It was supposed to be easy to get lost in the desert. I could walk on in this preliminary gloom, and in a few hours I would presumably be lost. Why had I come here with Inge? To find myself or to lose myself? Or had I come here to find her again? Had she come to find me?

Christ, it was cold. There was nothing romantic about the desert night. If this was supposed to be some sort of second honeymoon, then Inge and I had made a mistake. There was no way one could feel tempted to loosen one's clothes. The cold rose up from the ground and penetrated the bones.

I would have liked to have walked further from the camp, but I could not risk getting lost. Also, I needed tea, or something to revive me. In the desert, survival mattered more than sensuality. It over-rode my poetic whim, my need to walk on and get lost.

For the remainder of our trip into the desert there were two dominating sensations: the sensation of soreness during the day, as our legs were chafed and our muscles abused by the strange gait of our camels, and the sensation of cold at night, a coldness which robbed us of sleep.

Back in the village on the fringes of the desert, a wedding was being prepared. In the home of the bride's family, the women were busy cooking. Relatives had begun to arrive. The bride was sitting beneath the tattooist's needle, and a deal had been struck with a celebrated family of musicians who resided in tents at a well nearby. A day later, when Inge and I returned on our slow-moving camels, the wedding ceremony was in full swing. Our guide turned round in the saddle and grinned. Lines of ululating women advanced, and retreated in the white village square.

3

S O AFTER THE FUNERAL his mother paid for them to
fly off to Morocco. They flew there to get away from
London for a while. Not to forget. It was never going to
be possible to forget Dawn. They went to get away from
London and their London friends. For conversations and
relationships had become stressful. Everyone knew what
had happened. Many had expressed their condolences in
letters. And most began to behave in a way which inevitably seemed to take what happened into account. It
was not easy now to slip naturally into a conversation about
the Trobriand Islanders. It was no longer possible to discuss
the idea of the text. Getting away for a while might help
them to adjust, and it might also ease the situation with
their friends, for in a few weeks the event would feel more
in the past, and the fresh experience of Morocco might be
enquired about without hesitation.

Inge and Harry needed to be alone together. They
needed to see each other out of context, or in some context which did not immediately refer them back to the
event. It would be good if they could share something
again, go through something together – something quite
different to what had just occurred. Above all it was
important for them to get away from the house. For the
house had been bought for a song by Harry and utterly
transformed by Inge and her ex-husband. Quite the worst

of it was that the house still had a brand new feel to it. Its paintwork looked as fresh as it had looked at the culmination of Inge's pregnancy. It felt as new as Dawn.

THEY RIDE single file, away from the charred remnants of the fire. Their throats are dry, and their bodies feel stiff. The anguish of their loss is to some extent overwhelmed now by the discomfort of their immediate physical condition. Harry can only think vaguely of Dawn. He is more aware that his seat is sore in the saddle. He needs to grip with his knees in order to stay on, but his legs are so chafed it is torture to grip with them. He clings tightly to the front of his saddle. The day grows warmer, and the desert around them becomes a dazzle. He finds it difficult to keep his eyes open. How nice it would be to fall asleep. But the lurch of his camel prevents him from doing so. If he falls asleep he will fall off. Inge is faring no better. She sits hunched in the saddle, wobbling with each step forward and like Harry clinging to the saddle's wooden front. In a numb way, Harry reckons that he prefers this bodily stress to that shocked feeling of bewilderment which has to do with Dawn. Now he's keen for time to hurry on. His one wish is for their desert trip to be over. The thought of a bed is like some vision of Paradise. Yet it's hardly a week since he wanted to push time back – to crawl under the dining-room table and chase Dawn like a tiger again. He remembers how he felt winded. He remembers being unable to walk any further. And so he sank on his haunches, hands in his pockets, chin touching his chest. All of the stuffing knocked out of him. That non-physical pain had been worse than this. He'd remained a long time on his haunches like that, staring at the grass, the winter grass between his shoes. How long was it before he'd glanced up? Inge had stood beside him where he squatted beneath the black tree at Kew.

BEFORE THE SUN had risen far into the sky we had mounted our camels and set out again across the waste. It took many hours for any significant change to occur in the landscape. A large outcrop of yellow rock would remain in the same place in relation to us, despite our plodding past it. The camels dipped and rocked, as they strode driftingly forward with that languid movement of theirs which seems half way between a slide and a glide. The desert was silent. Occasionally Inge and I would try to exchange a few words. But as usual Inge's camel seemed to prefer to plod behind mine. She could only keep abreast of me by continuous kicks, prods and urgings forward. This hectoring activity interfered with our exchanges. For increasingly long periods she ceased attempting to converse and plodded behind me silently. Up ahead, our guide was silent also. He seldom turned to observe our progress, and there were no words of encouragement. The tribesmen who had been our companions for the night had all vanished, except for a boy who jogged along on foot beside the sliding haunches of the guide's camel. We passed between rock and sporadic tracts of scrub. There was little to do but hang on, watching one's shadow diminish as the sun rose higher in the sky. It became steadily warmer. The desert began to gleam. I pulled off my jersey and tied it around my waist. Having risen to it full height, the sun appeared immobile. Time seemed suspended. We plodded on in silence.

EVENTUALLY I slide into Rosemary and make love to her while Tom caresses us both in a slightly diffident way. Tom's softness is a disappointment. His lack of vigour makes me uncomfortable, for it seems like some comment on my own actions. To have touched this other man's hardness would have made me all the more excited. I would have liked to have guided Tom into Rosemary. Then I could have enjoyed entering her after Tom had found release within her. As it is, Tom has merely been looking on, stroking us as if this is a duty he feels somewhat embarrassed about performing. And now he has given up even doing that and just sits on the bed while we go at it.

I know that for Rosemary this is also a disappointment. Sure, I have serviced her myself with as much energy as I have been able to muster after my drinking and smoking. Her breath comes in gasps, and she has wrapped her legs around me, but I know that she wants to try another man's sperm, and that Tom has not provided her with the chance. Rosemary's promiscuity is not in the least like my own. She is not after release. It is hard to tell whether Rosemary is naturally promiscuous.

I climb on top of her and enter her again in the early hours of the morning. Perhaps I am fucking her while Dawn is fighting for breath. After this night, I go off sex for a while. Inge and I take a trip to the Sahara. I make one violent attempt on Inge's body, but that comes to nothing.

Then I fly to Manila. Being so far away from Inge, from our haunted house and our eagerly commiserating friends, I feel free to feel randy again. I feel randy in a hard, cynical way though. I just want to screw. Here, in the tropics, I'm surrounded by brown, pretty girls, who are forever smiling. The congress takes place in the reception room of the hotel where all the delegates are staying, and the girls are mostly students, recruited to look after the delegates. Each and every one of them is charming, and some of them write poetry and want to talk in an intense way about writing.

'But what is your poetry about?'

'Well, it depends. Sometimes it's not "about" anything. Why does art have to be "about" something? Sometimes I simply use words. I want to get away from poetry having to be about something.'

'But the husband of Kirsten, he wanted to speak about the rights of the Palestinians. He was shot many times in the mouth for his writing.'

'That was his struggle in his place in his time. I am from the West. My struggle is to break into abstraction – to give poetry the freedom to be abstract just as painting has been given the freedom to be so. Why should poetry be forced into a strait-jacket?'

It's actually cold inside this hotel – cold as an ice-box. I'm no longer in a sweat, except for an uncomfortable dampness where I sit.

'Yes, but the text you read us. That was not abstract at all.'

'Ah, but it was. I took all the possibilities of love-making and turned them into a system of permutations. I went about it in a strict, mathematical way. It's not so much the content as the changes which occur to the content.' (I wonder if the girls will notice a damp patch if I stand up.) 'Lift your ear off the meaning – listen to it as if it were a piece of systemic music.'

I talk and talk, but I cannot talk any one of them into bed. They sit in the lounge of the hotel with me or join me beside the swimming-pool. But few of them will drink, and none of them will swim. They talk and talk and smile, and that is all. It's frustrating. If any one of them wished to go further, nothing could be easier to arrange. My room is on the second floor of the hotel.

HIS FRIEND from the university sat beside him as one of the Marcos's aides drove them away from the airport. There were glimpses of sea to be had through the tall trunks of the palms, and they sped past thick-leaved bushes laden with exotic blooms. Incredible heat rushed past the open windows. There were bicycle trucks in the traffic, and many of the antiquated lorries were decorated with brightly-coloured scrolls of elaborate script. They cruised past long American cars. Tall hotels occupied the land next to the avenue, on the side opposite the sea. Each presented an elegant modern front above its set down porch and immaculately clipped lawn, upon which there was usually a sprinkler rotating.

'When our girls are naughty and get caught in the streets after the curfew, they are sent with scissors to trim the grass on the lawns of the President's palace. When morning comes, the girls are free to go.'

Harry indicated a thirty-foot-high fence, very smartly painted with white paint. It went on for a fair distance, following the curve of the motorway. Behind it nothing could be seen.

'What's behind that?' he asked.

'We call it the ghetto,' his friend replied.

IT WAS LIKE an exorcism. The boiling water spewed out of the kettle, over her ears, her cheeks, her throat. Inge pulled my arm.

TOM DRIFTS into the crowded, smoke-filled room. His blond hair has been lovingly washed and flows between his shoulder blades. Harry comes up with his arm around Rosemary. Rosemary is drunk.

'Hi, Tom!'

'Hello, Harry. Who's your friend?'

'This is Rosemary. Rosemary, this is Tom.'

'Hello, beautiful man.'

Rosemary reaches around Tom's neck, beneath his flowing hair. She fondles his nape and she kisses him.

'What's going on?' asks Tom.

'They're all avoiding me,' says Harry.

This is true. Harry's artist friends are avoiding him. The women among them are clustered around Inge, making a fuss of Dawn. Sometimes they glance at Rosemary. Rosemary sticks out her tongue.

'What did you think of the contacts?'

'They were good, man. I just wish I'd been wearing

some different gear.'

'Did you find one for the cover?'

'Yes, I think I did. Thanks for taking them, Tom.'

Tom begins rolling a joint. Only a few of the other guests will speak to them. Harry drinks some wine.

'So who is this woman you've landed on us?' asks their hostess; a sharp, scornful girl in rimless spectacles. She is nicely curved and could be attractive, but Harry thinks that she's very much into one-upmanship.

'That's Rosemary, Melissa. She's a bit fast for you artists, I'm afraid.'

'She's certainly moving quite fast at the moment,' murmurs Melissa. Rosemary is inhaling directly from the mouth of Tom.

'I hear you've left Inge.'

'Is that a question or a statement?'

'Well, Harry, I suppose the answer to that will become apparent in due course.'

'Maybe it will, Melissa.'

'I hear also that you didn't like my poem.'

'I quite liked it. I just didn't want to publish it, that's all.'

'So you didn't like it.'

'I don't think you've got as far as you may get. That poem's ok, but it reminds me of other people's work – mine for instance.'

Melissa bridles. 'I wrote it quite independently of you, Harry. I was just interested in separating words from the context of their sentences.'

'But you only managed it by their shape on the page,

not by anything dynamic going on among the words themselves.'

'I disagree.' She has gone quite red.

'So you disagree. I don't really know why you've gone into abstraction. Is it because that's what we're interested in on the magazine? You should feel free to follow your own direction. It won't work otherwise.'

'Yes, I can see how free you are. Free to leave your wife and your baby. Is that what freedom means?'

'Fuck off, Melissa.'

'God, you men are such shits.'

She moves away, and Tom passes Harry the joint. He takes it between his ring-finger and his little finger. Then he cups his hands together and inhales deeply. As he does so he catches a glimpse of Inge looking at him from across the room. Dawn is on her shoulder. Inge is wearing her orange dress – the one with the low Spanish flare to its skirt. Everything enlarges. He goes over and smiles largely at his daughter while Inge keeps her back to him. Inge is chatting with Susan, and Melissa has joined them. Otis Redding is singing "Mr Pitiful", and the women are speaking loudly.

'We should form friendships among ourselves and cut out men altogether.'

Dawn smiles at her father. She reaches for him from her perch. Harry makes faces at Dawn.

'The trouble with men is they possess no self-knowledge. They push outwards, not inwards. There's no desire in them to become more conscious of themselves.'

Harry makes pig noises. Dawn looks taken aback.

'It goes against the male myth, I guess. It's the warrior thing. They have to act rather than think. Women have learnt to think.'

'I expect thinking evolved in us during that enforced passivity we go through while suckling our young.'

Harry pushes his lower lip out with his tongue. Dawn does something rather similar but goes cross-eyed in the process.

'Yes, but despite that passivity, I think we're liberated by our thoughts. Men are stuck with their actions, you see. Actually, I think they need to be liberated far more than women do.'

'Yes, look at Harry. It's pathetic really. He wants to play with his daughter as if she were some little treat. But he can't take any of the responsibility for her. He can't stand the sight of her shit, you know.'

The record has come to an end, and a glass tinkles. Everyone is smoking cigarettes. Robert is telling a long and involved story to Yehudah. Another record is played, this time an oldie: Jackie Wilson singing "Reet Petite".

'Good evening, Harry,' says Laura, the large woman with the untidy stack of hair who was also at Dick's party. 'This crowd is a sight too intellectual for me. Would you care to dance?'

Harry likes her. Laura is large and relaxed. She throws terrific parties herself, crowded with boozy, unpretentious people.

'Go for it, Laura.' They dance. Somebody turns up the volume. Laura gives a North American whoop. Whenever he's around Laura, Harry feels that he can let himself go.

Their dancing becomes frantic. Her large breasts jostle each other inside her customary smock. Harry alternates the heels and the balls of his feet. Laura's precarious hair comes down. Finally Harry stops.

'Christ, I need a drink.'

The record changes to "Brown Sugar". Harry drifts away, and Steve begins dancing with Laura. In the corner of the room there's a table covered with half-demolished dips, the remnants of French sticks and a large number of bottles. Harry starts to pick up bottles. There are stubs everywhere. He goes on picking up bottles until he finds one with something left in it. Then he searches for a plastic cup which has not been used as an ashtray, and at last pours himself a drink. As he turns away from the table, he comes face to face with Delphina. There's a lot of din. He looks down at her lean, intelligent face and decides that he likes her very much indeed. Too much, probably.

'Soon you must come back,' she says in her East-European accent. She is quite small and somewhat hemmed in by the crowd, and Harry can only just make out what she says. Her large brown eyes gaze quietly up at him. He nods.

'Soon I will, Delphina. Have you got a drink?'

She nods and moves away. More guests arrive, and the vicinity of the drinks table becomes really tight with bodies. Harry shoulders his way through to the other room which remains a little less crowded. He catches a glimpse of Dawn's small face, fast asleep on Inge's shoulder.

People are beginning to unwind now, and several condescend to greet him or to touch his arm. He makes his way back to Rosemary and Tom. Another joint has been rolled. Harry puts his arms around their waists and begins smooching with them both. The joint is put in his mouth. He inhales. Rosemary removes it from his mouth and puts her lips to his. He exhales into her lungs, and she leans over and does the same for Tom.

Harry swallows some wine. He begins to speak in a loud voice, cracking jokes and saying scandalous things. 'Did you know that men are unable to think? Apparently they only push outwards – that's unless they're screwing, of course. Then they do push inwards, but only in a blind and thoughtless way.'

'Bullshit!' says somebody.

'No, it's perfectly true. They've conducted an experiment to see what people's blood does when they're feeling randy.'

'So what have they found out?'

'When a woman gets excited, all the blood goes from her legs, and when a man's turned on, all of it drains from his head. So the guy can't think straight, and the woman can't run away.'

Despite their sympathy for Inge, his artist friends begin to smile. Yehudah accepts a toke.

'So you're staying at Mario's now?'

'Just for a while.'

'He hasn't a chance in New York.'

'What do you mean?'

'His sticks, man. They're just too ephemeral. It works here because none of us are interested in purchases. Here we are interested more in concepts, as you know. But this is not New York.'

'So what do you think of his sticks?'

'Too much of a recipe, man. Too much of a recipe.'

Harry passes on the joint.

'Well, Rosemary, so what's your recipe?'

'Spunk is my recipe, Harry.' She laughs.

'There you are, Yehudah. You see, we've all got our recipes. You've got yours, I know. You never want the image, only the process that gets to the image. That's your recipe, my friend.'

'And what's your recipe then?' Tom takes the joint and inhales.

'My recipe?' said Harry. 'What's my recipe? Christ, I don't know. Abstraction through repetition, I suppose.'

'Harry, that's balls,' put in Rosemary. 'Your recipe is just screwing around.'

'Now that's what I'd call my Tantric recipe.'

'Tell us your Tantric recipe, man.'

'It's to go so far into pleasure you pass beyond desire. That's the way it has to be for me.'

'Come on now, Harry. What about higher values?'

'Look, if there are any higher values, or special states of being, or a raised consciousness, or anything like that, then I have to find it slap bang in the centre of the physical. The electricity for it has to be that of the body, that of the body, man. I want to pass through all the combinations till I'm beyond possession, jealousy, greed and so on. How's that for a recipe, off the cuff?'

They laugh and shake their heads and move apart. The drink has all run out. Inge comes over to Harry. There is a light in her eyes. She is looking very attractive. Dawn is still asleep on her shoulder.

'It was nice seeing you this afternoon.'

'Yes, it was good.'

'Are you coming home?

He pulls a face. 'I can't, you know. Got a sort of commitment.' He motions towards Rosemary with his eyes.

'Suit yourself,' says Inge. If she's hurt, she doesn't let it show. She moves away, and Harry admires her. He cracks a few more jokes. His eyes glint and he gives everyone a tight smile when they speak to him. Soon he sweeps out of the party with Tom on one arm and Rosemary on the other.

EVERYWHERE the scent of frangipani. Soft arms, soft, brown arms, holding out the garlands, tossing them over my head and arranging them on my shoulders. White, smiling teeth in smooth, brown faces, plump faces and heart-shaped faces surrounded by tresses of jet-black hair. Blue and crimson flowers in patterns on sarongs. And such laughter. 'Welcome! Welcome!' Wreathed in garlands, wreathed in smiles – wafting the scent of creamy petals mixed with the musk of armpits. Chanting, swaying and laughing there on the tarmac. Over my head go the garlands. And so I duck, and laugh a quizzical laugh, half-disapproving of all the fuss as I'm passed from hand to hand, squeezed against breast after breast. Well, I can hardly believe it. A corridor of swaying maidens waiting here for me. Chanting and swaying and smiling and singing. So this is what it is like to arrive at Manila airport.

Do they treat every new arrival this way, or is this welcoming party only laid on for the congress delegates or similar VIPs? Their hip-swaying, garlanded greeting reminds me of *The Mutiny on the Bounty*. As it happens, many of the maidens turn out to be students at the university's film-school – or so I learn later.

Of course I knew that I would have to accept the invitation. Whatever I may have said to her, my better mindedness is but an impulse. I'm not at all good at making sacrifices – not self-sacrifices, that is. They go against my philosophy. We had gone out and bought food and cooked, ourselves supper; and it was while I was doing the washing up that I returned to the subject.

'Inge?'

WHEN HARRY was eight years old, one of his mother's bitches had gone through a phantom pregnancy. On a rainswept evening she brought into the house three leverets. It was presumed that she had killed their mother. She carried them carefully up from the fields in her mouth and deposited them in the porch, one after the other. Then she whined and scratched to be let in. The night was lightning-flushed and stormy, and Harry and his mother sat up through most of it, helping the illusion smitten Afghan to nurture the leverets. Two of them died within the first few hours. The last leveret did better. She never learnt to suckle the bitch, but she would take milk through a pipette.

Within hours, she grew stronger and hopped dazedly around the carpet. Harry spent all his time with her when he was not in school. She slept in a box by his mother's bed. Harry would collect her from her box early in the morning and take her into his bed. She would, climb over the bedclothes searching for his face by stretching herself tentatively towards him, quivering at the tip of her nose.

WE DROVE in a cavalcade of cars to Imelda's villa. It was impossibly hot. We were all allocated luxury huts. I peeled off my sweaty clothes and changed into trunks. I swam in the largest swimming-pool I have ever come across. It was very deep indeed, and I felt like a midge as I kicked and trod water at the surface. None of the PLO wanted to swim, while Imelda's ladies-in-waiting seemed to think it somewhat provincial to actually use the pool. Even as I swam, I could feel the sun above the palm trees burning into my forehead.

The villa stood in a compound surrounded by tropical forest. The Soviets and the Libyans and the Egyptians and the PLO and the observer-delegates had all been given separate huts. These were roofed with straw, as befitted those of a tropical island. Each hut was smartly decorated and equipped with conveniences as well as accessories like packaged soap, neatly folded towels and a number of full-length mirrors.

Since my arrival in Manila, I had been sitting up far into the night, sipping dry Martinis and chatting, usually with Hernando, the President's script-writer. These late sessions compounded my jet-lag and by now I was dog-tired. An elderly American publisher, who had also been invited as an observer, was kind enough to offer me some uppers. Night had fallen. The riotous vegetation surrounding us was well lit; the jungle paths which led from the guest huts to the lounges and banqueting rooms of the villa being illuminated by elegant street-lamps with pearly, circular globes. Cicadas purred expansively. Things began to slide into each other; the lamps, and the rubbery jungle leaves, and the straw huts, and the men in suits and the generals and the ladies-in-waiting in their low-slung evening gowns.

Despite the uppers, I was still tired, and I began to feel light-headed. People spoke to me in soft voices, and I heard them as if from far away, as if from within a dream.

'Man, is this fantastic! Now if you were to try and find a place like this out on the keys it would cost you . . . '

'Oh, it has faults, his regime. But there are so many islands. Really, we need a strong man . . . '

'There was this guy down in Texas now. His daughter was getting married over in California. And do you know, he hired a fleet of planes and flew three-hundred guests from L.A. out to Houston after the ceremony, and then, when the reception was over, he flew them all right back again. And he'd had the planes painted kinda pink, see . . . '

'Yusuf Adwan. I know Yusuf Adwan. He is my great enemy. If he was here I will kill him. He is a traitor, Adwan . . . '

'Where is Hernando?'

'He is with the First Lady.'

'No he is not. He is with her favourite lady.'

'Oh, such a charmer, that man.'

I went back to my hut. I fell on the bed. The Valium would not let me sleep. How exhausted Inge had been after our trip on the camels. If I were looking for contrast, there could be none greater than that between our surroundings then and my surroundings now. Our desert hotel had contained the bare minimum of facilities. A sink, a table, a bed with metal springs and a lumpy mattress. Faded blue paint peeled from the wooden shutters. There was no soap. No towel. No mirror above the sink. From the wide, white square some distance away, the trilling calls of the women could be heard as they surged forwards and back, bending and swaying and stamping their feet, linked arm to arm in lines. We had caught only a glimpse of all this as we rode into the village on our camels. Too exhausted to stay and watch, we had gone to our hotel. Despite the noise, our bare room was heaven. Inge fell on the bed in the clothes she had worn for days.

4

THAT NIGHT, at his mother's farm, Dawn is quite violently sick. The following morning, they drive back to London. As soon as they get home, Harry goes up to the Oriental bedroom and rolls himself a joint. Then Inge comes upstairs to tell him that it's his turn to change his daughter's nappies. Harry tells her that he's too stoned to do it. Inge changes her nappies, but from now on she refuses to speak to Harry.

Harry wakes up the following morning with an erection. Dawn cries from her room, and Inge goes to pick her up. He glances at the clock. It is very early still. He curses and rolls over, but his hard-on gets in the way of sleep, so he gets up and puts on his dressing-gown. Still hard, he goes in search of Inge and finds her in Dawn's little room, also in her dressing-gown. She is bent over their daughter, changing her nappies. Dawn continues to wail.

'After this, let's go back to bed.'

He goes to the lavatory and then returns to the bedroom where he gets back under the covers. For some time, he lies fondling himself, thinking about Inge and their summer in Norway. Inge fails to return to the bedroom, and eventually he gets up again and goes to find her.

This time she is downstairs in the kitchen, holding the freshly-changed Dawn against her shoulder with one hand while she prepares a bottle with the other.

'Why don't you come back to bed when you've finished with her?'

Inge never looks in his direction.

He goes back upstairs and gets into bed again. After some ten minutes alone, he goes back down to the kitchen. Dawn has finished her bottle. She seems to have fallen asleep on Inge's shoulder. Inge is rubbing her back while sitting at the dining-table reading a book on the Vailala Madness.

'Come back to bed. '

Inge says nothing.

'Give me Dawn, then.'

Harry puts out his hands for Dawn, but Inge refuses to let go of her. A struggle then ensues; each of them pulling at their daughter. Dawn wakes and bursts into tears. Inge screams at Harry.

'How can you treat her like that?'

Delphina comes into the kitchen in pyjamas. Harry storms upstairs. He gets dressed very quickly. Then he takes his grass and leaves the house without looking at Inge or Delphina.

He arranges to stay at Mario's place while Mario goes to New York.

Christmas arrives. Harry refuses to come with Inge and Dawn to his mother's farm. Inge, Dawn and his mother come up to London to see him on Boxing Day. Harry agrees to spend an hour with them at the house. He is stoned when he gets there, and he plays with Dawn, but only in a desultory way. His mother makes a great to-do about how pleased they are to see him and how important it is to be together and how much Dawn has been missing him. Inge says little. She knows that Harry has been sleeping with Rosemary. Their newly decorated house looks very smart, with its downstairs rooms knocked into one, its green and yellow dining-room-cum-kitchen, its cork tiles and its kelims. They are both proud of their kelims, which they have collected together on trips to Kayzeri, Damascus and Tabriz.

AN OCCASIONAL cough could be heard. There was a shuffle of feet. Then a tape-recording began, of an organ playing *Jerusalem*. They all stood, staring blankly at the little coffin. What did it mean? It meant nothing. The music stopped, and the coffin slid out of sight. Then they trooped out of the chapel. A dark suited official came up to them and asked whether they wanted the ashes. No, they did not want the ashes. They would like the ashes to be scattered over the Garden of Remembrance. This turned out to be a very Hampstead Garden Suburb sort of garden reached through some brick arches. What did it mean? Harry's eyes lifted from his book as images from the funeral distracted him. He had flown from London to Cairo, from Cairo to Bahrain, from Bahrain to Bombay, from Bombay to Bangkok, and Gertrude Stein's *Geography and. Plays* constituted his only reading material. It was the kind of reading which seemed to encourage distraction. There was no thread to follow. The phrases returned you to your own thoughts.

You are so easily deceived you don't ask what do they decide what are they to decide?

What were they to decide? Or rather, what was he to decide? If Inge became pregnant again their friends would flock around them. 'Oh, Inge, I'm so glad. I'm so happy for you.' That was the middle class trap – the voiced happiness of your friends. Yet it was not so simple when there were books you needed to write; an urgency which commanded you. It was not that you were irresponsible: you acknowledged a profound responsibility where your talent was concerned. Your duty towards this upset your domestic devoirs, and somehow queered your more ordinary affections. Even so, there were other people, and how they said they felt, and how you thought they saw you. Yes, you could sell yourself into slavery, simply to please other people.

Harry sighed. A decision had to be made. And it was a decision which involved the feelings of several other people. For instance, there was his mother. She would be more than pleased if he were to get Inge pregnant again. But it was always the case that her approval of his actions constituted a hindrance. He hated doing what she wanted him to do. Merely to guess that it would give her pleasure was usually enough to put him off, even if it was just what he wanted to do himself. Yet in this case. In this case it was most important that he should avoid acting in a contrary way simply for the sake of it, and equally important to resist any clichéd attitudes to what anyone might think. What was he to decide? What did he really want? The wing drifted over islands, bays and lagoons all partially hidden by shreds of cloud.

NIGHT FALLS again. The camels kneel, and again we dismount. Again tribesmen materialise out of the seemingly empty desert. Meat is cooked. Tea is drunk. Inge and I sit with the tribesmen in a circle round the fire. We sit shoulder to shoulder. One of the tribesmen sings and then falls silent. And as the fire grows smaller we all huddle closer together. The cold can be felt on our backs. Inge is tired, and so am I. We are both stiff and very sore from our camels. Soon we retire to the tent. Again the night grows horribly cold; and it feels colder than the previous night. Perhaps we feel the cold more because our exhaustion is greater. The one blanket is hopelessly inadequate. We cling together, fully dressed, beneath this thin covering. The desert night becomes colder still; colder and colder and colder. The cold goes into the skin, then deeper, into the bones. It is far too cold to sleep. So despite our fatigue we remain awake, clinging together and shivering.

'Oh, Christ, Harry. We're going to die,' mutters Inge.

'Bullshit.'

'But it's cold,' she wails.

I grip her fiercely. And I begin rubbing her back with rough jerks of my palm. This whole situation irritates me. I feel angry with the cold, angry with the desert, with Inge, with myself. How could I have allowed us to get into this dangerous state? Fuck it. Fuck the cold. Fuck Inge. Anger is the only warmth I can generate.

A cold hour goes by. It is pitch black in the tent. We can hear the tribesmen shifting uncomfortably around the remains of the fire. A camel coughs repeatedly. Inge wraps herself around me. Another hour goes by, and now our guide crawls quietly into the tent. Inge clings closer to me, and I begin to feel tense. I cannot bear the cold. I swear at it between my teeth. I cannot take the weight of Inge's thigh lying across my pelvis. I cannot breathe with her hand on my shoulder, her arm across my chest. I try to push her away. It grows colder. A tribesman follows our guide into the tent. Shit. Inge and I are fighting for the blanket. Rolling away from me, Inge finds herself in the arms of the tribesman. She turns back to me, and she clings to me. I try to push her away again. A silent struggle ensues. I grit my teeth. I cannot sleep, I cannot even lie like this. I give Inge a sharp jab with my elbow. Inge releases her grip.

'THAT's bullshit.'

'It's perfectly true. Men are completely irresponsible. They make babies, that is, they contribute to the making of babies, but they won't accept any of the responsibility for looking after them.'

'I do have a career as well. I have to devote a certain amount of my day to writing. I just have to.'

'There's plenty of time when you're not writing.'

And so we haggled over our responsibility to Dawn. We were both fiercely keen to continue our careers. Inge was member of a women's group. I hadn't minded at first. But some of the women liked nothing better than deriding men.

Men are inadequate. They have no concept of foreplay. The entire history of the human race will have to be rewritten in order to take into account the struggles of women.

There was nothing I liked better than a debate. For the sake of debate, I would sometimes maintain that there could be a great difference between one man and another, just as there could be between one woman and another. Equally, every so often, a man and a woman might discover that they had a lot in common. The women in the group, which sometimes met at our house, took great pains to deny this.

How can a man have as much in common with a woman as another woman has with her? He doesn't experience periods. He can have no concept of what it is like to have a baby. He can't breast-feed.

I reckoned that I had quite a clear concept of what it was like to have a baby, having been brought up on a farm where the animals were forever giving birth. I had also been present at Dawn's birth and had written a poetic text inspired by Inge's labour pains. Some of the women enjoyed my writing and said that it certainly reminded them of what it felt like to have a baby. Others believed that to admit such a thing would have been politically compromising. There was one woman in the group who swore that getting a woman pregnant was tantamount to rape.

When I once remarked that you were likely to know what was different to yourself better than you knew yourself, my statement was greeted with howls of derision.

Honestly, men are just so arrogant. Look at Harry, he thinks he can know everything. How can he possibly know what it's like to be a woman?

I then made the assertion that it was difficult to know yourself because you were trapped inside yourself looking out. You never saw the whole, and you never saw yourself as others saw you. On the other hand, you did spend a lot of time looking at other people.

There was a chance that you might get to know these people – especially those to whom you were attracted. Of course it was possible to entertain delusions about them to, but the length of time you spent looking at them ought to count for something. Observation generally led to insight. People who fished got to know about fishes.

There he goes again, making out that a woman is an object. Women aren't fishes, Harry, you know. You're so far stuck into your chauvinism you can't see it yourself.

Initially Inge and I were strongly attracted to each other. We found that we had a lot in common. We both liked art. We liked making love. We liked intense conversations. We liked flirting with other people. We were neither jealous nor possessive. We enjoyed, the Arab world. We liked collecting Kelims.

But sometimes our niggling debates concerning the roles of the sexes turned into bitter wrangles. After Dawn's birth, these wrangles became quarrels. Neither of us felt very attracted by the other. In my opinion, we no longer believed that we had very much in common. Inge had become more interested in anthropology than in art. And I was obsessed by making love – or so I must have seemed. Sometimes love-making did not appeal to Inge. Our intense conversations were now rather infrequent. Dawn was all that we had in common – Dawn, and our Kelims.

Delphina came into the house. Initially she came in order to alleviate some of the pressure of baby-sitting. But I grew fond of Delphina. I began having intense conversations with her instead of with Inge. These conversations happened, during Inge's visits to college. Delphina's field was the history of art. She was there to look after Dawn while Inge was attending lectures, thus enabling me to get on with my writing. Instead I spent a lot of time sitting in the Oriental bedroom with her, discussing Crivelli and Carpaccio.

I kept very quiet about my fondness for Delphina. Yet the flowering of this intellectual, innocent and unmentioned friendship put as much strain on my relationship with Inge as did anything else – including the Rosemary affair.

After Dawn's death, an attempt was made to heal the rift which had come about between me and Inge. My mother felt that it was most important that we should become close again. She admired Inge, she thought her striking, and she wanted another grandchild. To this end, she urged us to go away somewhere. To be alone together. And she put up the money for us to do so.

Inge used to say that I never saw anything from her point of view. I maintained that my own point of view was the only point of view possible for me to have. Was this opinion at loggerheads with my assertion that one could only know what one observed? I glanced across at Inge who was staring out of the dust-smeared window of the bus. At the edge of the road there was a precipice. On one side one stared into space, on the other one was confronted by a wall of rock. Inge stared into space through the film of dust. Possibly it was our wrangles and our differences which preoccupied her.

Slowly the bus came down from the pass. We crossed a dry plain, and then the bus came to a halt in the wide, white square of the village on the fringe of the Sahara. In coming here we had got away from everything and everyone we knew. We needed to be together on our own. To find each other again. Like the Westerners we were, we presumed that the desert was a place where one could be alone. We spent that night in the village's one hotel, sleeping back to back, curled into separate balls.

In the morning, tea was served in small glasses. The sun formed ribbons on the bed, where its light fell through the faded shutters. Very soon we were dressed and in the street. We hired camels and a guide, and later that day we rode out of the village.

A FIGHT STARTED. Men leapt over the circular barrier into the pit. The vanquished cock was kicked, and trampled into the dirt. At the same time, the victorious bird flew up into the air to flap wildly over the seething crowd. Unable to maintain himself up there, he would land on a man's shoulder, perch on it until shaken off, and then rise, flapping wildly, into the air again. Some of the men were trying to separate the two owners at the centre of the fracas, others were either egging them on or joining in themselves. Brown, angry faces glistened now with sweat, and everyone was gabbling or shouting. Harry and the two charming boys who were his escorts rose from their places. Swiftly one of the boys took his hand, and they walked out into the traffic-reflected sunlight.

Laughing and raising their eyebrows, they led him through the streets. In that quarter there were shops which sold all manner of junk: scrapped auto parts, galvanised lettering, second-hand sarongs. Then they went inside a shop crammed with tourist bric-a-brac. Among less interesting, modern souvenirs, Harry came across a shelf of wooden figurines – saints and angels – in all likelihood pilfered from the many thousands of Roman Catholic churches which had been erected all over the archipelago. A primitive Madonna with an ample wooden skirt and a shape similar to that of a Manzu pope was very much in evidence.

Many of these objects were broken. Most of them were only heads, their bodies having been made out of fabrics which had long since disintegrated. Harry picked up the head of an infant Jesus. The entire bust was little larger than a walnut. It had been sculpted with great sensitivity and painted with equal care. The child had one glass eye. Its other eye was missing. Yet it was all done with such delicacy that despite the damage it remained a fine miniature portrait of a baby. A jewel in its small ear endowed it with femininity. The head was slightly inclined, and every nuance of the cheeks, the temples and the eggshell dome of the head had been touched upon by the sculptor. To Harry's mind, this was the epitome of a girl in infancy. Obviously she had been through the wars. The top of her skull and the back of it had been battered. The little nose was scraped, and the paint on one of her cheeks had been scraped away. It hardly mattered. All the life remained there in the particular angle of her face, the brightness of her eye and the pearly shading of her head.

Harry purchased this miniature. He took it back with him to the hotel and packed it carefully in his suitcase.

That night there was a reception for the delegates on the roof of another hotel. This was a rather grand affair. The table holding up the buffet was so long it was quite distinctly affected by perspective. On it were piled sliced meats, canapés, and a wide variety of exotic fruits: hairy ones, star-shaped ones, armour-plated monstrosities. Harry began to dance with a slender girl in a tight-fitting black dress, split at the side all the way up to her hip. She could have stepped out of *The World of Susie Wong*. Her eyes were almond-shaped and slanted, and her face was a wonderful oval. As she danced, her long black hair swung against her shoulders. Her legs were also long and stylishly set off by her very high heels.

She seemed amused by Harry. They talked and. laughed, and she twitted him about his lack of commercial viability. They danced again. The moon had risen above the sea, and the dark, mop-like heads of palms tossed among the streetlights below them when they leaned against the balcony to cool off. Sleek American convert-ibles slid by as they looked down, with suave men driving and bare-shouldered girls reclining on the back seats.

'Now if you wrote a best-seller you could have a car like that – a long American car.' She glanced at him out of the sides of her slanted eyes, with just the hint of a smile.

Harry attempted to kiss her, but she moved her head away.

'Why don't you want me to kiss you?'

'I don't know. You're kinda kooky,' she said.

Then she shrugged and flipped her smooth black hair over her shoulder as she walked away. Harry watched her hips and felt crumpled inside the suit he had worn since his arrival in Manila. Within a minute, the girl was dancing with the square shouldered official, also wearing a suit, who acted as minder to the Soviet writers and poets. The Oriental men wore collarless shirts of silk, except for some of the generals, while all of the delegates wore suits. There were plenty of girls, and all the girls were nice. But niceness only went so far. Harry picked up a drink.

It would have been great to have smoked a joint just then. He had not yet been offered any grass. It was difficult with the ladies-in-waiting around, and the generals. It was all so damned official. But it certainly would have been great to have got stoned in the heat of the night among such exotic surroundings. Yes, to have got stoned, and then to have sunk one's teeth into a fruit one had never tasted before, a fruit one could not name. It was never so good getting stoned in familiar surroundings. When he knew the scene too well, smoking only made him surly – languid and surly – as Inge said.

The dope seemed to sap his energy then, or that was how it was when he got stoned on his mother's farm. Things became larger, but they remained large, cold things. The desolation of the heath, where all the twigs were bare; the untidiness of the yard; slurry around the sheds, and the cows daubed with shit in the rented field, while the horses in their shabby coats were robbed of any sheen. He had felt melancholy on his last visit to the farm. He and Inge had just had another row – this time over whose turn it was to take Dawn out in her pram for a breath of air.

Harry had retired to the bedroom. The bed had been left unmade, and one of his socks lay on the pillow. He looked at his writing, where it lay open on the table by the window. It looked like nothing but writing: lines scrawled in a book. And these lines, what were they made of? Marks, they were merely marks. And writing at that moment seemed an occupation without any sensory value. Painting had colour, music had sound. Writing was nothing but a set of references. It seemed so second-hand.

Downstairs, Inge was stuffing Dawn into her winter suit, yanking up the zip and almost throwing her into the pram. Harry could be sure of all this. He had often watched the scene, and he knew how anger made his wife's movements abrupt. Next, the door would slam, and Inge would appear below, pushing Dawn at a swift rate in front of her. Harry sat down at the table and began to roll a joint.

THEY DRIVE BACK from Kew. In the large sitting-room of their renovated house the first thing which confronts them is the vacant baby-cage. On the way back they have stopped at the flat where Susan and Robert live. It has proved impossible for them to drive directly home. But now Susan and Robert are coming over, and Susan has already contacted Anita and Yehudah. Inge rings her parents as Harry opens the door to Robert and Susan. Then Harry rings his mother.

'Look, Dawn's dead.'

'What?'

'Inge found her this morning. It was like she had suffocated...'

'What have we done?' says Inge.

The lights are red. Inge is sitting in the driver's seat. Cars pass from left to right, from right to left. We are driving back from Kew.

'Christ, Inge, we've done nothing. It's not our fault. I've never heard of this, what's it called, cot-death thing.'

The tears roll down Inge's cheeks.

'I should have got up and looked at her.'

'And I should have been there. But I wasn't. And I didn't know. We can't go blaming ourselves.'

The lights change. Inge drives on. I stare at the streets as they pass. Cold, grey. Empty streets. I glance at Inge. Somehow she has managed to sniff back her tears. And now she concentrates on her driving. But she looks white, and her eyes are fixed, and she grips hard on the steering-wheel. There's nothing I can say.

Rosemary tried to stiffen Tom by sucking him. Images from the night come upon me, and I feel hot, but not from desire, from shame; shame that I can even think of such things at this moment in time. How long will it last – this time of abject loss, unending prospect of shame? There have been other times when I have thought, I am here now, and where I am seems interminable... sitting in a compartment of a train at night at an obscure junction – but this will pass, and I will look back at this moment and think how strange it is that the moment passed after all. Yes, it became the past. And yet, here I am, sitting in the car beside Inge on the morning of our daughter's death.

And when I think back my mind wants to push back further, further than the immediate fact of that. This is why I am at Mario's place. This is why I lie on top of Rosemary while Tom strokes my back. Shameful it may feel, but I kneel there on my knees between her outspread thighs. Then I reach round behind me and feel for Tom who is only small and. limp. I pull out of Rosemary and turn her onto her stomach.

SHE WOULD FOLLOW him when he walked away from her. But when he turned, she would scamper off across the lawn, laying her ears quite flat against her head, and then pause, with her ears cocked, to see whether he was giving chase to her. Obviously she loved the game, and she loved Harry. For his part, he loved his leveret with more fervour than the bitch who had brought her in; for the bitch was getting over her illusions of maternity and rapidly losing interest, though she never saw the creature as her prey. Harry loved his leveret more than anything else in his life. And he loved her more than he had ever loved anything before. Indeed, in the eight years since his birth, this was his first conscious experience of love. It was something of a wonder to him that he could love a thing so much. His strong feelings for the leveret were no doubt partly due to the bonding which had occurred on the night of her arrival, when she had lain helpless in his lap, and his mother had shown him how to feed her through the pipette. Another powerful factor was the leveret's loving him. Harry's mother was undemonstrative. It was not that she did not feel affectionate. She loved her son with a passion. But her husband had died during the war, and she had no wish to smother her son with her warmth and thus risk softening his personality. Harry understood little of this, but he did know that the leveret loved him. He knew by the way she came searching for him over the bedclothes in the morning. He knew by her willingness to play the chasing game. Harry had become her mother. He would have liked to have taken her to school. She was still so tiny that she would have fitted, into the pocket of his blazer. But his mother advised him not to take her, for the other boys might play with her too roughly. With reluctance, Harry agreed to leave her behind. And then all his school hours were taken up with a yearning to be home, to be lifting her out of her box, taking her down the stairs and outdoors, so that she could play with him on the lawn. One night, a week after the bitch had brought the leverets in from the fields, there was a terrible storm.

5

INGE BIT her lip. We were standing outside the front door, having just returned from the hospital in the taxi. All the way back we had stared down at our hands.

'I can't go in,' she said.

'Have you got your car-keys?' I asked, finding even this remark difficult to get out.

'Yes, in my bag,' she replied.

'Have you got it with you?'

'No, it's in the house.'

'Where did you leave it?'

'I don't know. On the kitchen table.'

I let myself in with my key. And I tried to avoid looking at anything as I made my way directly to the kitchen-cum-dining-room, where I found Inge's bag on the table. On my way back to the front door, I did not glance up the stairs, and I kept my eyes away from the baby-cage in the sitting-room. I just let myself out of the house and said to Inge, who was standing there on the pavement, 'Let's go for a drive.'

And so we had driven to Kew. We usually went to the gardens a couple of times a year, and Dawn had been there once, when she was very tiny. At that time, blossom had smothered the bushes, and its debris had lain scattered over the grass. Ducks had come waddling up from the pond to feed on the remains of our picnic. The sun shone for long passages of the day, emerging from behind the rare cloud that floated slowly past. Dawn sprawled on a blanket, bubbling quietly to herself. I can still see Inge bending over her to kiss her on the tummy. And then Inge raised herself and laughed, and stretched her arms upwards. Summer was always our best time.

Inge became silent and withdrawn during the winter months. I'm convinced that this seasonal mood-swing had something to do with her Norwegian blood. I've come across changeable women in the plays of Ibsen and the novels of Knut Hamsun. These emotional shifts are only natural in persons subjected since birth to endless summer daylight, endless winter night.

In summer Inge relaxed. She chose dresses which were sleeveless and which clung to her hips. Her arms and her throat grew bronzed, and her thigh would brush against mine when we walked in the sunlight, holding hands.

The summer before Dawn's birth, we had both gone to Norway, together with my mother, on the invitation of Inge's parents.

We stayed in some huts at the edge of a fiord. It was a time of lavish sunsets and twinkling water. Wet and glimmering there, Inge and I slid between each other's legs, playfully ducked each other or tweaked each other's parts as we swam in the fiord. Resin from the pines imparted a tang to the air which mingled with the fume from the heather. Birds floated from branches. The sun stayed late in the sky. Inge laughed and flirted with the English potter who lived with his Norwegian wife nearby. He grew his own grass, and both Inge and I got stoned on it. I wrote a great deal that summer. Most of the time we were happy.

Our only tiffs were to do with my own mother, who had come with us on the visit to Norway. Inge would relate her parents' criticisms of her.

'She never washes up, you know. Never. And she never even offers to do it either. And what drives my mother mad is that she also expects to be waited on hand and foot. Nor does she ever say thank you. She just sits there and takes her plate and eats. And she's always button-holing my father and asking him about this and that, but she never addresses a word to my mother, never a single word. She really is unladylike, you know.'

Too much of this would drive me from my writing and out of our hut. Once, after a particularly intense diatribe, I slammed the door on her and went off for a long walk over the rocks and through the pines fringing the fiord.

Inge relaxed in my company. But after a brief spell in the proximity of her parents she would become tense again and critical of my manner. Experience had shown that if she stayed with them for an extended period of time their attitudes would begin to get on her nerves, and she would swing back into sympathy with my views. Hamsun has dealt with the same sort of switches of liking and dislike in his novel *Pan*. It's the Scandinavian mistrust of a more Southerly hedonism coupled with an intense fascination regarding that same commodity. This ambiguous position is reinforced by the seasonal reverses. You never know where you are, I reflected, as I smoked a cigarette on a rock, contemplating the twinkling waters of the fiord and the bright sails of the dinghies scudding across it: sudden shifts of mood – exhilaration followed by melancholia and anger. But was I so different myself?

I had difficulty getting on with her father. My mother liked him because he was a doctor, and therefore a professional man. She admired that about him. I found him wooden. He had no sense of humour, and seemed to find it difficult to express affection, just as my mother did. Perhaps I was expecting too much of a father-in-law, never having had a father of my own.

Yet there was a humorous side to the man. Back in London, Inge and I used to laugh about the walkie-talkie he had bought in the Edgware Road, while visiting his daughter, which would enable him to keep in contact with his friend the police chief when they went Reindeer hunting together – it worked just as far as they could shout. Then there were the electric socks he had purchased in Harrods, which were to keep his feet warm when he went salmon fishing. He waded, into the river with them on, and some water splashed over his waders to give him a severe electric shock.

I smiled at this as I stubbed out my cigarette carefully and flicked its stub into the fiord. Then I made my way back over the rocks towards her parents' property. Through the conifers came the sound of methodical hammering. Inge's father was extending a summer hut's veranda.

THEY DRAW UP in front of a luxury hotel. As Harry steps out of the air-conditioned, car, heat is thrown over him like a thick, damp blanket. So this is the tropics. Now a doorman picks up his suitcase. Even without its weight to carry, Harry has broken into a sweat before walking the length of the carpet which leads to the entrance under a smart canopy. He is still wreathed in garlands of frangipani, though the creamy flowers have begun to wilt, and their scent has become almost sickly. Walking into the hotel is like walking into an ice-box.

LOCKED IN a flurry of wings, the cocks fly at each other's throats. I half-raise an eyebrow, a tight smile on my face. I've adopted the same expression when witnessing a bottle fight in a New York bar. It's good to watch something sharp and cruel: I feel that I'm throwing a secret V-sign at all the ultra-sensitivity of liberal, artistic London. Once Inge flew at my throat, rushed at me with her fingers bent into claws. I caught her wrists and told her to stop, but she kept on trying to claw at me, aiming to scratch my face. I bent a finger till it snapped. Then for weeks afterwards Inge went about with a splint on her finger. The women's group were up in arms, and the case against men was proved, at least the case against me was proved.

Dawn has turned blue, Inge's finger has snapped, one of the cocks is taking a beating. In the midst of things there are suffocations and breakages and sharp jabs from beaks, sharp as that jab from an elbow at night in the sheer cold of the desert.

And the next day we mount our camels and ride on. Little has changed since the day before. The landscape is much the same. The soft pad of our camels' hooves is the same, as is the dip and lurch of their stride. The only difference is that Inge and I are now more exhausted than we were. I can't rid myself of the sensation that our nights in the desert have been a sort of test, and that I for one have failed that test. Disappointment at my failure sweeps over me at intervals like spasms of nausea. I perch on my camel's hump, withdrawn into myself. Inge no longer attempts to push her camel forward so that she can ride abreast of me. No words are exchanged. The sun rises in the sky. We approach and then pass through a line of date palms, then a derelict hut made of mud. Again I feel stuck inside a moment. A prolonged moment which I know I will one day look back on, just as I now look back on the day we drove to Kew. The sun appears to be burning a hole in the sky. We plod on in silence.

WITHIN AN HOUR many of their friends were with them. Although their recently renovated house was not particularly dirty, the women began cleaning. They dismantled the baby-cage and tidied it away in the cupboard under the stairs. They took all the pots and pans, all the knives, forks and spoons, all the bowls and plates and dishes out of the cupboards and down from the shelves. The utensils were piled on the sideboard, the cutlery was heaped up next to the utensils, and the crockery was stacked beside the cutlery. Then they proceeded to wash up the lot. Also they emptied the bin with the last of Dawn's nappy-liners in it. Then they reached under the sink and put all that they found there on the newspaper they had spread on the dining-room table: the germ-killer and the hand sprayer; the clothes-washing liquid and the washing-up liquid; the powders and the aerosols; the poly-filler and the turpentine and the old brushes in jars; the window-cream and the furniture polish; the 1001 carpet-stain remover, the fabric conditioner and the 3-in-1 oil. Squashed out tubes of glue were discovered in corners and thrown into the garbage-bag. Then they scrubbed the cupboards clean. They wiped the shelves. They went into every nook and cranny beneath the sink, under the stairs, between the banisters; and in the bathroom, the lavatory and the shower. They hoovered all the floors and shook out the kelims. They removed all the sheets and pillow-cases from the beds and bore them away to the launderette. They removed Dawn's bedding and her waterproof sheet and folded these items away. They packed her romper-suits and her little shirts into a plastic bag and placed it at the back of a shelf in the dressing-room. They swooped everywhere, like a flock of gulls. Inge and Harry stood quite helplessly among them or sat hunched on the sofa, usually with cups of tea in their hands. Their friends cleaned and rinsed and dried the pots and pans. They did the same for the cutlery and the china. They rubbed the shelves dry and put away the bowls and the dishes and the plates. They sorted out the cutlery and placed each item in the appropriate compartment of the cutlery-tray. They shut away the pots and pans. And by the time they had finished, dusk had begun to fall. The entire house looked spick and span. It was like an exorcism.

IT WAS THE BEST bread we had ever tasted. Under its hard, warm crust, the flesh of the loaf was white and firm. Our appreciation of it was enhanced by the method of its baking. There was something miraculous about it: the loaf removed from the sand, born out of the fire. We squatted down to eat.

And I mused on the Phoenix as I tore apart my portion and put it into my mouth. Like the loaf, the Phoenix of legend was born out of desert fire. More precisely it was the Phoenix which caught fire. Its feathers became flames, and its flutterings blazed and then ebbed away into flickerings. But out of its own ashes came a fledgling. The womb burned but the young survived. I looked across at Inge. She glanced back and smiled.

'Mmm, it's good,' she said. We both smiled and nodded at the guide. He gave us a diffident grin in return and said something in Arabic. We shrugged then, and shook our heads, but continued to chew on the bread.

Phoenix-like were the fighting cocks I witnessed a week later. There was a white cock and a red one. The red one seemed particularly inflammable. He tossed his comb, crowed and plumed out his ruff while attempting to claw and strut. But his feet were held together within his owner's fists. Eager to be free, the cock's head darted between his own feathery thighs, attempting to peck the imprisoning hands. Then the owner would swing his clamped-together fists, and the cock would erupt into vivid flaps as he strove to find his balance. Certainly he was a fiery bird, and many bets were placed on him. Scalpel-sharp spurs were then attached to the ankles of both birds. But the fight could not begin till every gesticulating set of fingers had been registered by those taking the bets. The men positioned their cocks on the sandy floor of the pit and held them gently but firmly by their throats.

INGE IS LOOKING beautiful. She's wearing one of the cream gowns we brought back from Aleppo, and over it the striped coat with the flowing sleeves and the scalloped sides which almost reach her toes. It's a garment out of a Persian miniature. We found it in the great bazaar of Damascus.

Inge has bathed and washed her hair. For ages, she's been flipping and brushing her hair under the blow-dryer. Now there's a fine gloss to it. She sits cross-legged on a kelim spread on the cork-tiled floor of the red dressing-room, holding forth to Anita on the telephone.

'I asked him whether a kangaroo-man would ever eat a kangaroo. And really he looked positively shocked. My dear Mrs Harker, he said with his face very stern. I would have thought you'd have known that a totem would not be so much the first as the last thing on which a totemite would make a hearty meal. But what if the kangaroo-men were very hungry indeed? I went on. And what if there was absolutely no game around except a kangaroo, what would they do then? And he said, Well, Mrs Harker, I'm quite sure you and your husband worship your little girl. Now tell me, if he were starving, do you think your husband would put her on to boil?

Inge laughs at this. She's back to her slim self. No trace of her pregnancy remains. Through the doorway of the Oriental bedroom, I can watch her as she tosses her hair, confiding in the receiver. She looks wonderfully glamorous against the red shelves and wardrobes. I sit rolling a joint at the low table between the horse-shoe of beds. Its top is made out of tiles — the tiles we haggled for in Isfahan.

I spread a cigarette paper on the tiles and then open the finely decorated box given us as a wedding-present by the ambassador to Iran. From it I remove several pinches of grass, which I then place on the paper. The tiles are composed of thick, interlacing lines ending in blue or black florets arranged on a white ground. There are many ways of arranging their squares, and almost all of them produce symmetrical results. My obsession with permutations was distinctly aroused by them, and I tried a number of combinations before choosing the particular arrangement I stuck down on the table-top. Now I roll up the Rizla and moisten its glued edge. This I adhere so that the precious contents are firmly held within its paper cylinder – firmly, but not too tightly. If it's too tight, the smoke cannot be drawn through it. Now I perfect its top and its tail and glance again through the bedroom door at Inge. When she laughs, she lifts her head, exposing her elegant throat. Inge is beautiful enough to have been a model.

Surely such beauty is too conventional for a poet? Well, it doesn't bother me. When I was doing gymnastics, I met some particularly elegant young ladies. Inge is not quite as elastic as they were, but visually she's just as fine. And this is something I appreciate.

Now I smile as I hold down my first drag from the joint. It's like a scene from some Italian movie – *La Dolce Vita*, say. I catch Inge's eye. From where I'm sitting I offer her the joint. She pulls a very distasteful face then turns her attention back to the phone. I inhale again. Everything enlarges. Downstairs, in the lounge, Dawn rattles the bars of her cage.

TOM DRIFTS into the crowded, smoke-filled room. It's Harry who has invited him. Tom has just completed some photographic work for him – a portrait to go on the dust-jacket of his new book.

From the look she flashes, Melissa is quite put out by Tom's arrival. It's her party, and Harry has no business inviting his own guests to it.

Harry is in everybody's bad books anyway. Not only has he split up with Inge, he's also stolen Rosemary off Dick. In Harry's eyes, both these accusations remain open to interpretation. He is not sure whether the separation from Inge is any more than a gesture, and as for Rosemary and Dick, Rosemary was hardly Dick's property in the first place.

Tom's hair is Harry's main reason for inviting him to somebody else's party. It's the colour of an archangel's hair, golden rather than blond. He wears it very long and washes it every day. In rippling golden waves, it flows between his shoulders. He brushes it till it shines, and it moves about him like spun gold, conjuring up images of Leonardo and Rapunzel. It is more luxurious than the hair on any girl.

Harry wants him for Rosemary. In his mind's eye he can see the three of them together. To share Tom with Inge would be lovely, but Inge wouldn't participate now – she's into a different trip. Rosemary will do though. He looks forward to fondling Rosemary beneath Tom's golden hair. He's sure Rosemary will be game.

Harry feels very intense about such scenes, more intense than he feels about any deep experience with a single person. At the age of ten or eleven, he was caught with the children of some neighbours, naked in the bushes on the farm. Later, his mother took him to a tranquil corner of the yard and had a word with him.

'Sexual intercourse with the person you love is the most wonderful thing in the world. But otherwise it's a rather silly business, Harry, and playing sexually with people when you're not in love with them is very silly indeed.'

Harry's ears had burned, and ever since he has resented his mother's intrusion on anything that he considers his own private affair, while he has also set out to prove that his mother is altogether wrong. What does she know of sex – never having had it since the death of his father?

Harry positively enjoys playing sexually with people when he's not in love with them. He doesn't like to associate love making with love.

'Look,' he says to Yehudah. 'Love and tenderness, to me that's just soft-core pornography.'

Yehudah looks slightly uncomfortable. His eyes shift towards Anita who is choosing a record with Robert. 'I don't know what you mean.'

'To express tenderness to someone in your bed, that suggests politeness to me. It's not intimacy at all. Intimacy is not polite – it's when you feel that anything's permitted.'

Yehudah shrugs and moves away as Otis sings "Try a Little Tenderness". Harry acknowledges Laura's wave with a nod of his head. Through the cigarette smoke, the lights bounce off Tom's amazing hair. Rosemary has already begun to rub her body against him. Susan is telling a long and involved story to Delphina. Dawn's white face is like a damp petal on Inge's shoulder. The moody record changes to rock-and-roll as the Stones sing "Let's Spend the Night Together", and now a few people begin to shake their hips at each other. Laura comes up, but Harry does not want to dance.

He sips his drink and reflects on what he has just blurted out to Yehudah. Intimacy grows with trust, and love increases with increasing submission to indecency. It's a pity that Yehudah has shown so little interest in hearing more of this. To Harry, these are important thoughts, even if nobody wishes to hear him think them.

Lovers who really trust each other can watch while their favourite person is serviced by somebody else. To witness one's lover manifesting an appetite for another person seems especially intimate and a matter of ultimate trust. There is no confusing this freedom to be indecent together with Bourgeois, role-playing expressions of tenderness. To share some esoteric adventure is more intimate than any conformity to the sentimental images often associated with advertisements. And if these adventures are not love, then Harry is content not to love. Anyway, it's dangerous to really give one's love, and to actually feel tenderness is the first sign of such danger. Harry has learnt a long time ago how dangerous it is to feel tenderness towards anything.

He first began to trust Inge when she started submitting to indecencies – initially in a group, and then, with more mutual enjoyment, when they made love to their large friend Steve. The phrase, 'submitting to indecency' is one he has come across in an essay on the Marquis de Sade. But there's no direct sadism in Harry's dry permutations of the love-act. He is quite prepared to play a submissive role himself, should Inge so require.

Harry seldom offers much affection. He imagines affection to be somehow 'unmanly'. Having never had a father, his comprehension of what is or is not manly comes from his observing men at a distance. They seemed distant to him, as a small boy. Since he was deprived of the more intimate view available to children with both parents, this was how he saw them. And now, although he's grown up, he still imagines that a distance from tender exhibitions goes with being a man.

But Harry can be fun; and this excuses the rarity of his demonstrations. It is his sense of fun which makes him attractive. He can also be intense and is prone to button-holing people. Then they move away, just as Yehudah has done.

'It's not your views,' Inge has told him. 'It's the way you insist on holding forth. You never give a person room to think.'

Since Dawn's arrival, Inge has lost all interest in their indecencies with other people. She's only turned on when she has Harry to herself.

Harry finds it difficult to come to terms with the change in her. When he suggests an adventure now, Inge shakes her head.

'I know you don't want to, but tell me why you don't want to.'

'I just don't want to anymore.'

'But you used to like our adventures.'

'That was before we had Dawn.'

'It's a bit hard on me. I still like the idea of adventures.'

'I find it all a bit childish now.'

'It's not childish. Why should it be childish? I think we should have an adventure.'

'Don't push me, Harry. I can't stand it when you push. You begin to remind me of those dreadful men I used to work for. They would always push. Just remember this. I'm not your personal assistant.'

Harry knows that Dawn is responsible for the change in her. Of course he cannot blame the change on Dawn. But where she is concerned he does sometimes experience a spasm of irritation. Very young ladies are unladylike. They are more or less helpless, and their needs must be dealt with by adults. For a country boy, Harry is strangely fastidious where his daughter is concerned. At first he was repelled by the visibility of her toilet. This repugnance was largely brought on by his fear of dropping her or of getting the procedure wrong. Since she's grown a little older, he has also begun to experience feelings of tenderness towards her. But those towards whom we feel tenderness are inevitably hostages to fortune. Harry realises this and tries to keep his tenderness in check. He has started to smoke a great deal of grass. Grass helps to keep him remote.

But Inge is not attracted to Harry when he is stoned. Coming on top of her rejection of adventures, her rejection of him when stoned leaves little room for manoeuvre. Harry smokes all the more frequently now. And the occurrence of intimacy has become all the more rare.

Inge is cold towards him and warm towards Dawn. Harry has taken up with Rosemary and continues to find occasions for indecency, although Inge is now absent from these proceedings. Recently there's been a row, and Harry has gone to stay at Mario's flat in Belsize Park. He's brought Rosemary to the party at Melissa's place in Ladbroke Grove, and he's invited Tom along as well. Inge observes their antics with appropriate *sangfroid*. Most of their friends cut him dead. Nevertheless there is Dawn. Across the crowded room, she crows at her father when he pulls faces at her. Despite herself, Inge smiles at Harry and shakes her head. At that hectic party there are overtures and an opportunity for a reconciliation. But it's all so difficult with everybody present: the friends they never touch, and some of the throw-away people as well. The situation is too difficult to resolve at this moment in time, and as the party draws to its close, Harry makes his exit with Rosemary and Tom.

They bundle into a taxi. It's a long way from Ladbroke Grove to Belsize Park.

THE SKY CRACKED, and jagged forks of lightning struck the lawn. The house shook. Harry was anxious for his leveret. There had been storms on the night the bitch had brought her in. He had felt then that fear of the storm had killed her brother and her sisters. But this new storm was the worst of all possible storms. There were great bangs when the night flashed, and the dogs all whimpered in their baskets. Harry could not sleep. He got up and went into his mother's room and said that he wanted to look at his leveret in her box. But his mother told him not to stand about in his pyjamas. She sent him back to his bed.

Morning came in a grey, continuous drizzle. Harry went to his leveret. The tiny creature was trying to gulp for air. But her lungs had collapsed. Her pink mouth opened and shut, but this was a last vain effort. Soon she was dead. It was fear of the storm that had killed her.

INGE RELEASES her grip. She removes the pillow. Our daughter's face is blue. I struggle awake. I am in the dark. All thoughts are possible, I realise, and this horrible thought is one among the many possibilities generated by the event. Such possibilities rise up in my sleep like permutations in a systemic poem. Maybe she this, maybe she that, because of such and such, because of something else. This is the hell of it. This is the snake biting the arm of its owner. Now we are exposed to these possibilities, lost in a wilderness, tented from the sky − nothing between us and the hard desert ground. We have not murdered our daughter, and yet we feel like murderers. We feel that way because she has died.

Inge releases her grip on me during the night. I have jabbed her with my elbow and caught her beneath a breast. She grunts with pain and rolls away. But I haven't been able to breathe under her weight, her thigh, her clamping arms. I haven't been able to breathe. And Inge does it because I shake my head. Because I leave her so obviously at the party. Shake my head, abandon her and Dawn, sweep out of there with Rosemary on one arm and Tom on the other. How does she feel, alone among the last of our friends, with most of them aware of how I've snubbed her?

Or God has done it, although there isn't a God. But if there were, He might well have done it. A God could easily have disapproved of my actions. And if there is a God, He is a retributive God. He is the frightful cold responsible for these thoughts; grotesque variations on ordinary thought, emerging jumbled from dreams it is too cold to continue dreaming.

I half-wanted to turn back as we lurched into the street after that party. I felt bad that I had left Inge and Dawn to get home on their own. But Rosemary nibbled my ear, and her mouth was very hot. Tom embraced us both. In the dank night air our breathing mixed and became a common cloud. Then Melissa slammed the door behind us. The three of us hailed a taxi.

'WHAT I WANT to say to you guys is that sometimes, well, you sort of get an idea that something is going to happen. This goes on a lot in societies which use their dreams, you know.'

Susan had written a book on dreams. She sat opposite us in the extra clean, renovated house. All trace of our baby had been tidied away. Susan had lived in England for a long time. She was an American by birth.

'But what I want to say is, you sometimes may get an idea that something is going to happen, but that doesn't mean that you should go around blaming yourself for anything.'

'Of course there is no one to blame,' I said.

'I don't think I had any idea that anything was going to happen,' said Inge. 'But I heard her cry in the night, and

I was just so tired I didn't bother to get up and look at her.'

'Oh, come on, Inge. You weren't to know.'

I stared into my tea.

'You see, that's what I mean. You sort of get a vibration that something might happen and then it does. It's sort of weird. '

'I don't really buy all this,' I said.

'But if I had got up, maybe she wouldn't have. God, I don't know. Maybe she wouldn't have got into that state.'

'I didn't get any vibration,' I said. 'Inge, you weren't to know. I never heard of cot-death before. I never heard of it.'

How many times that day had I said that?

The door-bell rang. It was Robert, Susan's husband, back with a large bottle of scotch. He found some tall glasses in the kitchen and placed them on the dining-room table. Then he unscrewed the cap. The amber fluid poured from the mouth in swift, hiccoughing glugs.

6

GAIN SHE LIFTS the kettle to pour steaming, scalding hot water over her cheeks. What is she trying to punish in herself? Is there a trick? Has she learnt to withstand the scalding heat? Or is there no trick? Is it all just punishment? Punishment for shame or pain? The water streams off her face, hotter than any tears. Then she rubs her face and puts the kettle on to boil again. Harry hasn't cried over his daughter. He sort of collapsed in the bathroom, but he hasn't cried. He has cried over a girl he once knew, who rejected him. But that was self-induced. In those days he was steeped in romantic poetry. The tears felt sensuous then; a delicious abandonment to a form of grief that was more a celebration of aloneness. His worst tears, his truest tears perhaps, were spilt over his leveret. How many years ago was that? It doesn't matter. He can still feel how scalding hot they were. They were painful tears he prefers never to experience again. Tears jerked out of him from his guts, forced on him by some insistent images. Yes, she would flatten her ears. She would stagger across his pillow, stretching her neck towards him, trembling at the tip of her nose. She would suck eagerly on the pipette. She would follow him when he walked away from her.

IN THE MORNING there is nothing. No water for tea, and no bread. It seems to take a long time for the guide to dismantle the tent. Once it is packed away, they walk over to their kneeling camels. Slowly they climb into their saddles, and the camels rise, one after another, their back legs straightening first. Each gets finally onto its feet with a lurch that throws the rider forwards. There is no glamour about them anymore. They are not 'ships of the desert' but surly, recalcitrant brutes, always happy to bite a shoulder.

This morning, Inge's camel is particularly loath to rise, and she is almost too exhausted to curse it into action. At last it staggers up from the dirt. They ride single file, away from the charred remnants of the fire.

It felt as new as Dawn. Inge and her ex-husband had done a great job while Harry had been away. A wall on the ground floor had been knocked down, and a rolled steel joist had been set in its place beneath the ceiling. Instead of two pokey rooms connected by the corridor which also led to the back extension, they now had one large, open room, down into which the stairs descended. This area was connected by a sliding door to the dining-room-cum-kitchen which took up the whole ground floor of the extension. Dawn had her bed in the small room on the landing above this area, though for the first few months Inge preferred to have her sleeping in the cot next to them in the Oriental bedroom or in the red dressing-room adjacent. The bedroom itself was just about as sumptuous as any chamber in the seraglio at Topkapi, and the bright red dressing-room connected it to the bathroom. All this was on the first floor. On the floor above was a shower cubicle, Harry's study and the guest bedroom. Inge kept her books and her writing-desk in Dawn's little room. The entire house was extravagantly decorated in the primary colours Inge's ex-husband enjoyed. He was an artist who had never sold his paintings to anyone but Inge and her parents. When Harry visited Norway, he was quite taken aback to discover how many of the man's large, busy abstracts had been purchased. He did not mind, of course. But if only her parents had been as interested in abstract poetry as they were in abstract painting.

This was not the case. Very few people ever seemed interested in abstract poetry – apart from the poets who wrote it and one or two extremely conceptual artists. Inge's ex-husband still owed Inge money, despite the sales, and his decoration of their house was his way of paying off his debts to her.

Delphina occupied the guest-room. She had recently separated from her husband who was a translator. He dealt with the literature of her native Eastern-European country, and Harry had met them both in the Mid-West. After the translator's residency was over, the couple had come to London.

ONCE THERE, they had decided to go their own ways. Harry had invited Delphina to stay, and to help with Dawn instead of paying rent. Inge had started her course by this time, and she was glad of the help since Harry was not to be relied upon.

Their guest was skinny and small, with brown hair and big brown eyes. She had prominent cheek-bones and an intense, waif-like expression. Of course Harry was attracted to her. She was an art-historian, and she and Harry would have long, conversations together while Inge was at college and Dawn was asleep. Sometimes they talked about Carpaccio, and sometimes they talked about Caravaggio. Delphina was very intelligent. She knew a great deal about her subject, and despite her stumbling English and her Eastern-European accent she could put across what she knew with remarkable clarity. Her legs were slim and rather well covered with hair.

It was pleasant to discuss art which was not the latest thing. It made a change from his conversations with Robert, Susan and Yehudah. Then there were times when their talk drifted towards other matters: the shortcomings of Delphina's husband, Harry's philosophy of marital freedom. They would sit together around the table in the Oriental bedroom which was often used as a lounge because of its horseshoe-shaped arrangement of rug-covered beds piled high with cushions. The more they sat there the more intensely they talked, and the more intensely they talked the larger Delphina's eyes would grow.

Nothing happened however. Somewhere inside himself, Harry recognised Delphina as a threat. She was more intelligent than Inge, he felt, and he was always fascinated by intelligence. When he took up with Rosemary it was almost as if he did so to ward off the frank power of Delphina's intelligent eyes. It was quite obvious that Rosemary cared more for his sperm than she did for him. She cared more for sperm than she did for any man. He knew that she would move on to milk juice from other testicles, and that he was no more than her immediate supply. She in

turn was his caprice, and as such she never really constituted a threat to his relationship with Inge, for all that he
played out the role of splitting-up with her and flaunted
Rosemary in her face.

With Delphina it would have been different. And
when Harry left the house and went to stay at Mario's, it
was not entirely because he wished to claim independence
from Inge. He was also distancing himself from Delphina,
for had he moved closer to her in the Oriental bedroom
there might have been serious consequences. For her part,
she was grateful for the accommodation and loyal to Inge,
who had after all agreed to have her in the house. She also
got on with Inge. Harry was aware as well that she was
definitely not a throw-away person. There were considerable problems about becoming attracted to a true friend,
for such attraction, he knew, would always tend to grow
stronger and could last a very long time.

In the pre-Rosemary days, before Harry's dope-intake
became a major source of irritation, the three adults and
the infant lived in the renovated house in a state of uneasy
happiness. They would cook together and eat together, and
Harry was gallant to both the women. The thought of certain possibilities made his mouth go dry and kept him
awake at night. What should he do? Delphina felt attracted.
Inge was looking beautiful.

MY ROOM was on the second floor of the hotel. Any girl
interested in being alone with me could walk with me up
the two flights from the lobby, or we could take the lift.
But if I were already in my room, it was unlikely that I

would receive a surprise visitor. At the head of the stairs, on my floor, stood a stocky policeman in a short-sleeved shirt. The hair on the back of his thick brown neck was cropped short. I noticed him first as I stepped out of the lift, following the man with my suitcase. I registered the prominent holster. Nobody would be able to come up alone and enter a room unchallenged. Presumably there was a similar guard on every floor.

Once alone in my room, on that first day in Manila, I showered and shaved and then got dressed again in my suit. I was jet-lagged but had no desire to sleep. My wide window looked down on a large swimming-pool surrounded by deck-chairs and parasols. The pool was deserted, and its deck-chairs were vacant. During my stay, nobody ever swum in it but me. There were a couple of sweet, brown girls who would accompany me to the pool's edge. They never went into the water.

Having dressed, I went downstairs. Miranda Cruz, my spider-monkey friend, was sitting in the lounge chatting to a Japanese lady in a golden wind-cheater who was a famous beat poet. Shoulders were hugged and cheeks pressed together. Noriko lived in Japan, although she'd been born in Canada. I'd met her in the Mid-West at the same time as I'd met Miranda.

Drinks were ordered. I was introduced to a very soft-handed, light complexioned old man with wrinkled, Oriental eyes.

'I live in New York, at the embassy,' he told me. 'I do not like what I see here, and I do not care what I say. But I am too important to be shot or thrown into prison.'

'Garcia is our most celebrated poet,' Miranda leaned over to explain.

'And so I am an unofficial exile. But this is of my own choice. I do not like the Philippines. Me, I like New York.'

The hotel was full of writers. There were journalists from Egypt and from Libya and several members of the PLO, including the Danish wife of their recently assassinated spokesman. Then there were two or three authors from Moscow, a poet from Siberia (he hadn't been sent there – he lived there and wrote poems about its considerable natural beauty), and finally the dour Soviet overseer. I was given an identity button and informed that I was to be called an observer-delegate. Noriko was also an observer-delegate, although she was from the East. The business of this writers' congress was to cement ties between the Russians and the Middle-East. Garcia, Noriko and I had been invited to lend the thing a little credibility. The interests of ASEAN were being accommodated by the regime as well, and there was also a 'Flying Tiger' office on the same floor as my room. The congress was basically an excuse to air propaganda while completing undercover deals between officially hostile nations.

Cars kept rolling up in front of the hotel as other delegates arrived on subsequent flights. If a car did not contain a delegate it was more than likely to contain a general. In the space of an hour, I met more generals than I had seen hot dinners.

'YOU SAY THAT. And I don't push, and then it never happens.'

The teat boils on the stove. Inge takes the bottle which already contains several scoops of milk-powder. She fills it and shakes it and goes upstairs. Harry mooches over into the kitchen area. He wants a cup of tea, but there are no cups washed-up.

'It's your turn to do the washing-up.'

When did the haggling become bitter, and when did the niggles turn into wrangles? And why has he always to put things so extremely? He leaves off staring at the dirty cups and goes upstairs. Inge is feeding Dawn in the Oriental bedroom. Harry goes in there and sits down. He stares at his hands. Sporadically a drill chatters in the street. He looks up at Inge and Dawn and then looks back down at his hands. Delphina comes down from her room and goes into the bathroom.

So what about Delphina then? She and Inge got on. It is on the tip of Harry's tongue to say it – to suggest a new adventure. Yes, but he never says it. He doesn't want Delphina associated with a row. He can guess what Inge would say. She would argue that Delphina is not a throw-away person. Dawn pushes the bottle out of her mouth and doesn't want to suck.

'Come on, Dawn,' says Inge.

But Dawn refuses the teat.

'Oh, come on,' says Inge again. She's reached the end of her tether.

'Don't shout at her,' says Harry.

'You get her to take it then.' Inge plonks Dawn down on the bed, leaves the bottle and hurries out of the bedroom.

Harry goes to the door after her. He stands in the doorway and shouts.

'Don't expect me to feed her.'

Dawn begins to wail. He picks her up and carries her with him back to the doorway.

'Inge, I'm not going to do it.'

But he goes back to the bed and gets her bottle. Still Dawn refuses the teat. She is too busy crying now to concentrate on the milk. Harry sighs with exasperation.

'Come on, you. Come on.'

It's important for both of them to forget scenes like this. What is the use of remembering? It will not bring her back, and the scenes have no bearing on the event. They need to get away. And soon after the funeral they fly to Marrakesh.

THE THREE of us hail a taxi. Once inside, Rosemary begins snuggling up against Tom and playing with his long, golden hair.

'Mmm, you're like an angel.' Her tongue flicks him on the corners of his lips. He turns to her and puts his hand on her knee. The taxi pulls away from the kerb. Rosemary's long woollen dress rucks up as she grips Tom's leg between her thighs. Now she starts to push her tongue far into his mouth. The taxi lurches round a bend, and I'm thrown against them. Rosemary laughs. I put my hands underneath her dress. My palms slide smoothly up her thighs, over her hips and then up her ribs. I rub her nipples roughly, and then begin to pinch them. As usual, they are hard. She turns more towards Tom, but at the same time she pushes her bottom at me.

The taxi rattles on through the night. It's a long way from Ladbroke Grove to Belsize Park.

THAT NIGHT they slept in a tent under a single blanket. High above them, in the black depths, billions of stars burned coldly from their fixed positions in the firmament. Only occasionally would a shooting-star break the stillness, and then its streak could not have been more brief.

None of this could be seen from where they lay under the canvas. They tossed on the hard ground, and the vastness they knew to be outside only made the tent seem the smaller. They lay in their narrow darkness, and Harry felt that they had been in darkness even while they sat astride their camels. In the bus they had looked out through the dust-smeared window from a darkness they carried inside them. Was there, even before what had happened to Dawn, a darkness which had enclosed them? How could he say? How could he know about Inge? He lay in his own darkness outside her. He did so now, and he had always done so. Even when they were making love, this had been the case. You were in your own darkness despite the fact that part of you was deep in someone else. Well-rounded characters might people novels. In life you stared out at the world from behind your eyes, from within your inner darkness. And so you were blind when it came to knowing what was going on inside other people.

Harry could only know of his own movements, think his own thoughts. There was a darkness about the way things happened as they did. And he happened as well; he did things and said things and was often as much in the dark as to why he did what he did as might have been any external observer. He knew still less about Inge. He could not know what had happened on that final night of his absence from their house. This was an indictment of his behaviour; an irrevocable indictment. On that night he had not been there. He had not even been there. And how could he know what Inge felt about that? For since that night they had been elaborately gentle with each other. Now she lay beside him, and he could feel her shivering in the cold. But how could he know what she wanted? Why should she say what she really felt? How could he tell if what she said she felt was in fact the case? What did 'in fact' mean, when feelings changed so often? Why should he know the answers to these questions about Inge when he could not answer such questions about himself? So dark was the blackness. So blind did he feel, both inwardly and outwardly.

Did he want another baby? Did she? What he wanted was the freedom to write without obligation to others. What she wanted was to succeed on her course. And yet they had had a baby. The summer before last they must have felt differently. People said that the first months after a baby's birth were always the most difficult. Brand-new mothers and fathers were often on the verge of madness. It was so hard to adjust to the new roles. This was why babies sometimes got burned by cigarettes or punched or thrown down the stairs. Maybe there was something biological about it. The greed of love was not so far removed from the greed of hunger. He remembered a hamster which had repeatedly eaten its babies. And his mother's Afghans would sometimes lick the new litter clean so vehemently that the weakest runt would get damaged.

Before its birth, he thought to himself, the baby is a notion. It's a dream possibility. We see ourselves showing off in our new definitions of ourselves. Having a baby is something which it's permissible to boast about. But the prospective parents have little awareness of the actual nature of their new life. They don't realise how much of their time will be eaten up, how many of their own activities will be curtailed.

He and Inge had loved Dawn, but now Dawn was dead. Did they need to create some new vessel so that they could pour into it all the love that remained in them? Or could they stop loving now that the reason had passed away, stop loving and get on with their professions?

Well, Harry thought, if you're going to have a child, you ought to decide that you will love that child very much indeed; certainly enough to make sacrifices, because in all possibility you will be asked to sacrifice part of your own identity – perhaps the convivial atmosphere at the pub, the hour's chat which relaxes you after a day's work, or it could be that crucial session getting your own art done instead of serving others. The new role diminishes the earlier one. When you have a child you have to be prepared to let a few things go. You have to decide it's the baby that counts. Otherwise why have one? Harry could see now how the wish to be a parent could easily get mixed up with one's own vanity. All too often it was erroneously perceived as an inflation of one's self-image. Or it could be the last gambit in a progressively tedious game, a ploy to keep the relationship together: a final ploy, coming after the ploy of buying a house, and coming after the ploy of getting married.

But what was uncertain, he realised, was whether such doubts were whims, customary for most couples to experience at intervals after the months of nappy-changing and bottle-making; after teething had begun and already been the cause of interrupted sleep. The sudden ending of their daughter's short life threw such doubts into a garish light which vastly expanded their shadows. Perhaps these thoughts were whims. Death gave them emphasis. Their black shadows covered your face like thick canvas, through which the stars could not be seen.

Your waters broke or you lay beside your wife in a wet bed. You went to the hospital, and one of you experienced hard work and perhaps considerable pain while the other sat holding a hand or maybe reading aloud from some hopefully distracting book. In Harry's case, he had read Inge a magazine article on Disneyland as she strained and attempted to distend.

Then you went home with a child and learnt to support her head. You showed her off to your friends. Perhaps you got pleasant sensations while your nipples were sucked. Perhaps the time spent nursing your baby could have been spent researching into indigenous education in Africa. But then you lost your milk. You had tiffs because of the new strain on your lives. You kicked your heels in the house and began to suffer from claustrophobia. Then you woke up one morning to hear that your daughter was dead.

Blankness at first. It's odd wearing a new role, but the dismay is greater when the role is suddenly snatched away.

They woke in separate houses. Inge discovered Dawn. She rang Harry. They met at the hospital. It was too late for Harry. Too late for him ever to see his daughter alive again. He would not see her dead. He had not experienced her birth because of a simple biological fact. And because of a gesture towards independence he had not experienced her death.

His last glimpse of her then had been at that crowded party, clinging to Inge's shoulder.

When they returned from hospital, Inge had not been able to enter their home. And so they had driven to Kew. By a black tree he had squatted on the grass. He had stared at the grass, and the grass had been grass. He had been too blank for grief. He had felt, this is freedom now. But he'd known that he could never admit that he felt that. Blankness by day, blindness by night. Blindness within, blankness without. He remembered a French novel. How the character had stared at the trunk of a tree, and how the trunk of that tree had had no meaning. Now he stared at the black tree. The tree was black. He rose to go. They drove back from Kew.

AND SOON after the funeral they fly to Marrakesh. The jet lifts them away from the dreariness of the English winter. They touch down in the hard winter sunlight of North Africa. The still, sombre figures of their relatives and friends at the funeral dwindle in their minds as they walk into the bright, noisy crowds milling through the bazaar. A fat lady plucks at Inge's sleeve to show her the bracelets on her wrist and the jewellery beneath her many chins. Inge tsks as she lifts her head in refusal. It's easy to get back into the swing of it: the offers, and the denials which are mere feints, well-worn ways of bringing down the price. Men approach them with carpets, and Inge looks at these and begins to haggle with the men. Then she looks at Harry and shakes her head. As usual they are more interested in kelims, but there are no kelims as such, only thin, pile-less woven mats. These are decorated with tightly-patterned, horizontal bands. They are unlike anything they've ever seen in the Middle-East. And they might look nice draped over a chair or a sofa, but Inge soon loses interest in buying them. She does not want to haggle. They move out of the bazaar into the main square. Gypsies are performing here, in the circular centres of crowds. There are men with snakes, and acrobats, and many men with drums.

I DID NOT cry very often. I was more likely to get angry. I could fly off the handle at the drop of a hat.

Tears were too painful, or else they were faked. But anger was my forte. I had rows which made *Who's Afraid of Virginia Woolf* sound like Barbara Pym. Sometimes I started a row simply to stoke up my boiler. Anger was energy. It brought things out in the open. It set your heart racing and raised the level of electricity in the atmosphere.

I had rows with men. I had once jumped up and down in front of a very large black man. There was an old building whose rooms were used as studios by artists. Not long before, I had put on a show during a day of events there.

The show was based on a text I had written on the labour of child-birth, and I had invited pregnant ladies to come and read the text or perform in the birth event which accompanied the reading. Many women turned up, all more or less resembling pears. Some revolved slowly in the long room where the event took place, sporadically enclosed and then revealed by performers holding aloft king-sized sheets attached to tall wooden Ts. The sheets were striped red, white and blue, and the wooden Ts were painted crimson. I had bought these sheets in the mid-west, taken by their American colours. Three of these nicely-striped sheets would form a triangle around a revolving pear. The triangle would itself revolve slowly, then open out and glide in a line towards another pregnant woman. Meanwhile others sat on cushions, rotund as female Buddhas, reciting the text in chorus:

'Now. Now there. Now there the width. Now there the width the breath. Now there the width the breath soon.

Now there the width the breath soon breathing now the letting out. Now there the width the breath soon breathing now the letting out about to be.'

Abruptly, all this was obliterated, by a battery of African drums. With hindsight, I realised that this must have created an interesting theatrical collage. At the time, I was furious. I felt that all *my* labour was being deliberately sabotaged. A timetable had been agreed, and the drums had started up long before schedule in the courtyard.

I jumped up and down in front of the largest drummer.

'Racist!' I kept shouting.

But for all that, my best rows were with women. These

went like clockwork. You wound the women up until they broke down. Then there physical fights and tears, and sometimes the delicious relief of making up by making love, the women damp and softened after misery. Anger was my domestic theatre. I used it for effect, and I benefited from its catharsis. And often so did the women – unless it went too far.

Where did my anger come from? I had always fought with my mother, who liked to get her way. I was never punished physically by her though, and so my tantrums went unchecked. Rows were a family tradition. My mother rowed with my grandmother, and my grandmother rowed with her cook. There was no grandfather, and there was no father. I grew up among quarrelsome women whose rows were furious and then forgotten about. Giving vent to my passions was thus a habit formed in my childhood, and later it seemed only natural that women should be the target for my spleen.

Inge's pregnancy calmed me down. It awed me rather. I went away to the Mid-West, and when I returned Inge was massive. Because the situation was about to change there seemed little reason to voice any dissatisfaction with the present. I was anyhow pleased to be home. We fucked carefully, me coming at her from behind. Afterwards we would sprawl on the cushions in the Oriental bedroom, sipping mint tea from the small, shapely glasses we had brought back from Turkey.

'What are we going to call him?'

I SIT WITH the small, furry corpse cradled in my hands. Tears fall from my cheeks onto her fur. Gently my mother lifts my leveret away from me.

'You'd better get dressed for school now.'

'I don't want to go to school.'

'I think you'd better. It will help you to forget.'

Still crying bitterly, I go to my own bedroom. Everything feels broken. It takes me a very long time to get out of my pyjamas and into my school uniform. My hands feel almost numb. I'm still crying as I try to eat my Rice Krispies. The tears fall into them. It's awful crying. It hurts me in my stomach, and it makes me choke as I try to crunch. I push away the bowl. I don't cry very often.

7

THE AMBER liquid pours from the mouth in swift, hiccoughing glugs. Soda is added, and ice. The drinks man is a black American in bow-tie and tuxedo.

'How you liking it here?'

'Fabulous,' says Harry dryly.

'Yup, it's a fabulous place alright.'

The drinks man mixes a cocktail in a silver shaker. He shakes it softly in time to the maracas which provide a rhythm for the combo on the dais above the dance-floor. The svelte night remains warm, and the moon shines brightly down on the white canopy of the tent. Dark ladies in low-cut gowns emerge from the villa and cross the lawn. Meeting others coming the other way, their heads move together briefly, messages are murmured, then they separate. Most of the delegates are drinking. Whenever the combo takes a break, the sea can be heard crunching away at the beach beyond the palms.

A brown general with a crew-cut comes over. He nods briefly at Harry, and then leans on his fists as he inclines forwards to murmur something in Tagalog.

'Right away, Sir.'

The man in the tuxedo bends under the white table-cloth. Then he straightens and hands something to the general. Whatever it is, the general slips it into his hip pocket and goes away.

Harry sips his scotch. 'How long have you been here?'

'Came over with the military some years ago. Then I liked it so much I settled down. Best thing I ever did. You one of these writers?'

'I'm a writer.'

'What do you write?'

'Mostly I just write.'

'OK. Does it sell?'

'Nope.'

''Bout time you did something that'll sell. All these guys here, that's what they're into. Everyone's selling something.'

'Everyone?'

'Every single one, friend, and I include myself. The generals are selling. And Imelda is. And all these Soviets and Arabs. They're all selling, you can bet.'

'Well, I guess that's true.'

'And you ain't? Well, you better get your act together, boy. Selling's what it's all about.'

'Not to me it's not.'

The drinks man shrugs. He busies himself at the table, refilling the ice-bucket, packing away used glasses.

'Hey, you oughta write something on the Philippines.'

'Maybe I should.'

'There's plenty going on here, boy. You got a knock-out here.' The man glances at the guests on the lawn and grins.

'Love and intrigue at court, you mean?'

'Don't say I said so.'

Harry turns away to wander onto the dimly floodlit

lawn. Bushes with enormous blooms reflect the glow from the lamps. Finding it impossible to sleep, he has re-joined the party. It's fairly late. The moon rides serenely through the sky.

It's not a bad combo, and it's a neat dance-floor, but nobody is dancing. The drink is limitless, but nobody is that drunk. Imelda has retired to some inner sanctum of her villa. Over by a palm, a few Egyptians are talking with many gestures to the rich Texan. Every so often, a lady-in-waiting will ask Harry about his last visit to Liberty's or to Harrods. Despite all the expense, the party is a desultory affair. There are too few guests to make any impression on the enormous compound. Perhaps court-life is a continuous party anyway, or at least one reception after another. It's apparent that people are apt to become very blasé about it.

Noriko comes up to him.

'Hi!'

'Hi, Noriko. How goes it?'

She kisses him, and they touch glasses. He admires her red turban and the blouse she is wearing which is covered in sequins. Her legs fit with aplomb into a pair of gold lamé slacks. She sways on crimson high-heels.

'Oh, I so tired now.'

'Yes, it's non-stop, isn't it?'

'Non-stop, yes. But is very bad as well.'

'Is it?'

'Very bad. Imelda, you know. She make me very angry. This morning, when we visit landing. "This is where MacArthur liberate the Philippines." She say it like she very glad, remember? I think very rude of her. She forget. I am Japanese. I think of boys too frighten to come out of jungle. If one die, you know, Harry, if one die the others eat his body. They was very frighten. Even after armistice. Philippines very bad for Japanese that time. You know, Harry?'

Harry nods. A breeze rustles the palms.

'I'm going for a leak,' he says.

'OK. I find Miranda.'

Harry walks along the paved length of the swimming-pool. It's illuminated from beneath the water. The sheer size of it is daunting. There are no high jinks here. There are no squeals or guffaws, and no one is given a drenching in full evening-dress. If this is *La Dolce Vita,* Filipino style, then it's a very staid affair. There are swimming-pools by every hotel and in every compound. Vast swimming-pools. Private, rectangular lakes. But nobody ever swims in them. Nobody but the rare ingénue visitor such as himself. The limpid, light-blue water lies absolutely still.

Steps lead from the pool through the palms, down onto the beach. Here the palms hide the moon, and except for the brilliant stars it is very dark. He stumbles onto the sand. At least he should be able to say that he's pissed in the Pacific. He unzips his fly. Helmeted silhouettes rise suddenly in front of him. Harry can just make out the muzzle of a machine-gun.

A soldier barks something in Tagalog. Harry turns away and pisses in the other direction, not in the ocean but onto the sand. Then he re-ascends the steps. It's a warm, breezy night. The Valium or his sleeplessness seems to have affected his physical sensations. He feels silky all over. Soft. The warmth of the tropical air seems to caress him under his shirt. It's a shame that the women are so unwilling to make love. Of course, there is always Noriko. But she's old enough to be his mother, and besides she's told him that she's only attracted to black GIs. But, as for the natives, they're all of them charming teases, each and every one of them, from the nubile student to the buxom lady-in-waiting. And the more they set out to charm, the more their behaviour irks him. And then they're so bound up in their court intrigues and their Catholicism. Such a shame in such a setting: tropical, breezy darkness, convenient huts in the jungle, drink and the scent of affluence.

As he stands by the side of the large, still pool, he slips his hand inside his shirt and begins to brush first one nipple and then the other.

'You have the skin of a girl.'

A BROWN GYPSY woman wearing a red bandanna on her head was squatting by a low fire. Why had she attracted such a crowd? A black kettle was simmering on the fire beside her. Drums clattered to the right of Harry and Inge. They stood on tiptoe to see over the heads of the other spectators. Whenever the black kettle began to steam, the gypsy woman would lift it off the fire and hold it near her face. Then she would tilt the boiling water out of its spout so that it poured over her brown cheeks. She would put the kettle back on the fire, fill it from a flask, and then rub her cheeks swiftly while she recited incantations. The water would come to the boil again. Again she would lift the kettle to pour steaming, scalding hot water over her cheeks.

'I DON'T WANT a name anyone can shorten,' Inge said, and I agreed.

'But I don't want one with any sort of connotation – like Sean.'

'Most names do have connotations.'

'That's right. I suppose it's more a question of what the connotation is.'

'Peer is a nice short Norwegian name.'

'Yes. I like Peer. I've always liked the story of Peer Gynt.'

'What if it's a girl? I wouldn't want her to be called Jane.'

'I quite like Jane.'

'You like Jane. I'm not having her think we called the baby after her.'

'I don't like Rose.'

And so it went on, the subject being returned to at intervals, right up to the time of her birth. I looked up from my Gertrude Stein and stared at the blue through the port-hole. A rose is a rose is a rose.

Had she been a boy she might have been a James. My leveret had never had a name. She had died before I could give her one. And Dawn's life had been so short that much of my thinking about her was bound up with the prelim-inaries, all that had gone on before her arrival: Inge's stom-ach enlarging, the choosing of her name, and being given the baby-cage by Anita.

Why did we call it the baby-cage and not the play-pen? It was one of those phrases Inge used that just stuck – a Norwegianism. But Dawn now. There was so little to remember her by . . . and so much of my memory taken up with preliminaries, and now with images of the funeral.

It was much the same with my leveret. I retained only one or two images of her vital moments. In my mind, these images were contained within a small globe of absolute happiness. But then the globe was never allowed to remain intact. Later memories smashed it. The sky cracked, and jagged forks of lightning struck the lawn.

'WHY DO YOU have to do it so often?'

'Why shouldn't I do it?'

'You shouldn't, when it makes you remote.'

'It does not make me remote.'

'Yes it does.'

'No it doesn't.'

'Well, you seem remote to me.'

'Maybe I want to be remote.'

'Why should you want to be remote?'

'I don't know. I want to be remote.'

'You want to be remote from me and Dawn?'

'Inge, I just want to smoke.'

'It makes you remote. It makes you remote.'

'So what? I want to do it.'

'Well, it makes you surly.'

'What?'

'It makes you surly as well.'

'Why should it make me surly?'

'I don't know. It does though. I can tell.'

'I don't give a monkey's whether it does. But why should it make me surly?'

'Well it does, Harry. It just does.'

AND BECAUSE OF this I thrust at her all the more savagely. Because she's so dry. Because it hasn't worked. Because it's all such a wash-out. I force myself to push it into her because I'm indifferent now. The electricity has ebbed away. There's no chance of me coming at all. I know her body too well. How strange that you can be lying on top of someone, both of you naked, your rudest parts in contact, and yet remote, untouched by that. Knowing each other too well. For there's nothing about her that's unfamiliar. Nothing to fire the imagination.

For me, sex isn't a feeling brought on simply by physical titillation. Thought matters just as much. Sex is a work of the imagination. I ejaculate with my head.

Love-makers can be divided into the Ernests and the Raymonds. The Ernests are for Hemingway. Sex is a matter of experience. You come because she begins by giving you a hand job, or because she paddles you, or because she makes her back-passage available. The Raymonds read Roussel. For them, the experience is neither here nor there. You can be caressing your pillow. What counts is the ability to sustain the illusion. If you can imagine that your pillow is Mata Hari or that you're love-making in the basket of an air-balloon then you're well away.

I've got a foot in both camps. I require a work of the imagination that's rooted in personal experience. In ideal circumstances, I'll begin by whispering another woman's name into the ear of the woman I'm embracing. The one I hold, or who holds onto me, has to become the other in my mind. Next I'll ask her to call me by some other man's name. I want sex to take me out of myself, and the more unreal it seems the more excited I get. For mostly I want to forget myself and forget who the real she is. This is what makes our coupling new. The reality of the person you're with is not the essence, nor is it essential to treat your pillow as if it were a real person. What's crucial for me is to find a real person who can be treated like a pillow.

I realise that it's all too easy for people to misinterpret this desire. But why is reality such a healthy thing to be stuck with? Reality is wooden – wooden lovers going through their solid, stolid motions. And why should fantasy be relegated to some private fetish object? To share one's most intimate dreams with another person – even when those dreams deny the other's presence – to share such a denial demands an honesty of admission which can only be built up through trust. This is love itself, although it may seem to wear the guise of indifference. At least it posits a way to cope when the novelty goes out of making love. At least it suggests a strategy when faced with the problem of staleness. There's nothing I like better than being treated like a pillow by someone else. I adore hearing other people's wishes voiced as they straddle me or lie beneath me. It feels very exciting to be called by another man's name.

Of course it's no good treating your friends like pillows. With your friends you talk about art or anthropology. Friends have difficult edges and sharp corners. It's no use trying to pummel them into shape. This is why Inge and I divide our acquaintance into people we keep up with and the throw-away people. Throw-away people are lovely to fuck. They're affable and tender, and each is attractive in some special way. True, you have little in common. But that's why you fuck. Our real friends take umbrage all too easily. Every one of them is useful, either to my career or to hers. They mount exhibitions which one is expected to attend, and they write books which are obligatory reading. In return, they read my books, though they rarely buy their own copy. They also read Inge's papers. These sort of friends matter far more than the others.

And so they're the first to be contacted. And within an hour most of them are here. They scour the house of ghosts. They seem to understand. They offer advice based on their reading of other people's researches. They cite the Hopi Indians. Inge and I sit down in one place or stand up and revolve slowly and then sit down somewhere else as our friends flash past us, tidying this away, putting that upside-down to dry. It's all rather bewildering. I sit hunched on the sofa, while Inge sits upright on a chair in the dining-room part of the kitchen. By now the house looks immaculate.

BY THEN THE HOUSE looked immaculate. Darkness had set in. They were drinking scotch with the last of their friends, liberal doses of scotch – no ice and no water. Susan sat cross legged on the sofa, leaning forward as she talked. It sounded as if the Hopi had the answer.

By now Harry was leaning against a radiator. Susan elaborated the Hopi's point of view. Eventually he went upstairs. Nothing made sense. Everything felt broken. He fell down in the bathroom. Inge came upstairs. Harry tried to stand up and fell against her. He felt dazed.

'I don't know,' he said. 'I don't know.'

Inge held him. He sagged.

'Oh, my dear,' she kept saying. 'Oh, my dear.'

A SLOW SMOKE rose into the twilight. Inge wanted to walk a short way from the camp. I kept her company. The desert was fading into the evening's cool. Bushes merged with the rocks behind them, and the rocks disappeared into low hills.

I glanced at my wife. She was wearing a khaki shirt and khaki slacks. Now she brushed back her hair to reveal the high cheek bones of an Indian. I admired her long throat and her small breasts, her slim waist and her wide hips. What a striking woman she was. I was smaller than her, but more agile. Where she was stately, I was deft. People said we made a nice couple.

Now her dusty face looked tired. It had been a long day; the culmination of a harrowing period in our lives. But now we were alone in the desert. Now we could look for peace within ourselves. Inge sniffed.

'It's a shame there are no real dunes,' she said.

'Isn't it just? I was really looking forward to seeing some.'

'It's typical, you know. We've come all this way for the desert, and now it's the wrong sort.'

'Still, it's not so bad. The camels are fantastic.'

'Christ, but I'm sore!' she remarked. 'I can hardly move now. How on earth am I going to manage tomorrow?'

'It'll pass,' I assured her. 'Isn't it still? I haven't heard a bird.'

'Did you see that sign for Timbuctoo?'

'Wasn't that weird? They measure the distance in days. I wonder what it would be like to go all the way.'

'I don't think I could take that.'

'Strange to be so far from any road. I wish I'd scored some grass in Marrakesh. This would be the place to turn-on.'

'Why do you have to smoke so much of that stuff?'

HARRY UNLOCKS the door and ushers Rosemary and Tom into his friend's flat. Rosemary lies down on the low bed with Tom while Harry fusses with the lights. Tom says, 'Ah,' as Rosemary bites his ear. Harry unzips Tom's trousers and pulls them off him. Rosemary holds Tom's face in her hands. She kisses him on the lips and then tousles his golden hair. He begins kneading her breasts while Harry slides his hands beneath her dress. She wears no panties, but this he already knows from his explorations in the taxi. His lips move over Tom's hands and onto her breasts. As usual, her nipples are hard. Harry begins to go hard. He puts his face between Tom and Rosemary and kisses them both. Their three tongues touch. Tom is slightly unshaven. Rosemary's lipstick can be tasted on his tongue. Harry slides a hand across Tom's chest and then down to his stomach. Rosemary moves up the bed. Tom removes her dress. Harry's hand slides under the elastic at Tom's waist. Tom remains small and slack. He moves down the bed, away from Harry's hand, and begins kissing Rosemary's stomach. Harry goes between Tom's legs. Tom goes lower on Rosemary's body. As Tom begins licking her private parts, Rosemary twists about. She sighs and pulls up her knees. Harry pushes his nose against Tom's thighs. He rubs him and sucks him, but nothing seems to make him stiff. Rosemary turns around and begins sucking in Harry's place. Harry moves up the bed. He holds her buttocks and kisses her behind. Then he rolls onto his back and gets beneath her. He begins sucking her while she continues sucking Tom. But Tom remains limp. Rosemary turns around again. She presents her pelvis to Tom. Then she spreads her legs and tries to insert him into herself. At the same time she begins to suck on Harry. Then Harry goes behind them and tries licking Tom from below. Nothing they do can harden him. It's rather a let-down. Perhaps Tom has taken too much marijuana. Perhaps Harry's presence puts him off. Eventually Harry slides into Rosemary and makes love to her while Tom caresses them both in a slightly diffident way.

IN THE MORNING tea is served in small glasses. Wrinkled stripes of light fall on the bed through the blue wooden shutters. The celebrations are over, and the women have fallen silent. There is no sound of drumming.

It is some time before Inge and I step out of the hotel with our shoulder-bags and cases. But now there is nothing in the village to hold us. We walk slowly to the centre of the wide, white square, which is at this hour quite deserted.

Once at its centre, I upend my suitcase and sit down on it. From my shoulder-bag I take out a book by Gertrude Stein – which I proceed to stare at. Inge places her suitcase next to mine. She stands a few yards away, silent. The sun causes a dazzle on the ground.

About twenty minutes later we are joined by two Arabs. They are stiff-jointed old gentlemen with wizened faces, and they wear ill-fitting suits and decorated caps. No words are exchanged.

Then a man and a woman come along; the man in a white gown with a shawl over his head, the woman swathed in a medley of tinsel-decorated fabrics. The man is laden with cases and bundles, while the woman drags a toddler by the hand and supports an eight month old baby on her shoulder.

I glance up but then return to my book. Inge looks away across the square. The baby has a very bad cough.

The square is so wide that it takes a long time for those who approach to enlarge. And now the day grows warm. Heat haze affects the periphery of vision. After a further quarter of an hour the group at the centre of the square has grown to some ten persons.

At the distant edge of it, sporadic signs of activity are now visible. A kneeling camel is being loaded up with what look like oil-drums outside one of the low, white houses. But this small event is happening too far away for the eye to catch much detail. It is also distorted by the heat. The group at the square's centre wait in a silence broken every so often only by the baby's wretched cough.

At long last the bus arrives. We climb aboard. Inge seats herself by a window. I settle in next to her and continue staring at the pages of my book.

We say nothing to each other. Inge does not read. She gazes out of the window as the bus rattles across the plain. This arid place shows signs of cultivation but manifests hardly any response to the attempts which have been made to get crops from it. The bus passes a woman bent over a hoe, working alone in a field of stones. We drive through foothills covered in meagre scrub, and then up, winding our way along ledges cut in the brown crags; the bus negotiating each hair-pin bend with much grinding of gears.

Now the rattling jolts of our progress make it impossible even to pretend to read. I leave my book on my lap. I glance at Inge whose head remains turned away from me. The baby's cough can still be heard above the noise of the bus. There is a precipice below us.

What does Inge want? It's so difficult to tell. She seems as ambiguous towards me as I feel indecisive about her. Is she waiting for me to be totally positive? 'Why did you stop?' she said. So she did not want me to stop. But I felt that I should stop. No, it was less decisive. A sudden faint-heartedness seized me. Even as I did it to her I could see freedom like some floating island moving further away.

Then I stopped. And the island drifted back so that I could feel its incline under my toes. And I told myself that as far as it went I would only do it if she made it absolutely clear to me that that was what she wanted.

And that's how it is now. Because it's up to her. She just has to be positive.

We reach the top of the pass and begin to descend. Perhaps Inge feels no more positive about it than I do. It's true that she's not on the pill — nobody would expect her to be after what has happened. Yet it's essential now to go beyond expectations. What does it matter what our friends feel or what my mother wants? It's quite likely that Inge can also see that this is an opportunity for us to be free, even if she can never admit it. Whether she can admit it or not, this is our chance to be free of each other, free of the responsibility of it all. Inge can pursue her career. She's now at liberty to do her field work in Egypt if she wants, or she can go further afield. It's only the conventions of society, the accepted notion of what a marriage is, that puts this pressure upon us. After all, we only got married in order to buy the house. There was no other way that I could get my trustees to release my grandfather's money. Then one thing has simply led to another. And now the conventional notions are urging us to try again, to sort things out, to set our domestic ship on an even keel.

Yes, and it's dreadful. What's happened is dreadful. And having another is the only possible homage we can make to the small life we remember. Yet at the same time, both of us are ambitious. Inge wants to reach the top of her field. And I want to be thought of as *the* poet of our age. Our incautious actions in the heather were the impulsive outcome of that happy summer after our wedding. And now fate has given us the opportunity to re-think. If we are prudent now we may realise our individual dreams. Inge can become an anthropologist, and I might really get somewhere with my writing. Surely she feels as I do about these matters?

The bus rolls to a stop in Marrakesh. We book into the same hotel as we stayed in only a few days earlier. But now we're only booked in for a night. Our flight back to London is scheduled for tomorrow morning.

Once in our room, Inge unbuttons her khaki shirt.

She's not wearing a brassière. She sits on the bed and pulls off her shoes.

'Harry,' she says. 'Can you get these off me, please?' They're so tight, and I'm still stiff from the camel.'

She unzips her slacks.

I kneel at her feet, and she gives me the faintest of smiles. I take the bottom of one leg of her slacks and yank it over her heel as she raises herself from the bed. Then I do the same for the other leg, and the slacks come off. Except for the unbuttoned shirt, she is now down to her panties. She leans back on her elbows on the bed.

A few strands of pubic hair escape from the sides of her panties. Her thighs look very warm and smooth. I glance up, and she is still smiling at me. But I get to my feet and avoid her eyes. She raises her knees and pulls her panties off herself. I move over to my suitcase and unlock it. Inge peels off her shirt I begin rummaging for another book.

Inge gets off the bed. She takes a towel from her own luggage and goes into the bathroom. I can hear her running a shower. I find the book I want and begin turning the pages. It's not Gertrude Stein, but it might as well be. I just can't focus on the lines. Inge starts to sing in the shower. I sit down on the bed.

I WAS NOT in tears for the sake of the people watching. These were tears which spilt and would not stop. I was crying because I could not stop. I had cried on the way to school. All the way, I had walked slowly in tears. Then I went on crying as the other boys jostled their way into the hall for Collect. And I cried through Collect and then through all my classes. When the other boys asked me what was wrong, I found it hard to reply. Once or twice I managed to say, 'My leveret.' They nodded seriously enough. But they did not understand. A master asked me what the trouble was and only got a mumble in response. The master walked away with a shrug. I was actually trying to stop. I was trying hard to stop. But just as my eyes would begin to dry, images would return to me, especially the image of her scampering after me and then running away when I turned to give chase. This was an especially sweet moment at the time it occurred, because she seemed so lively, and I could be quite jubilant about how my mother and. I had brought her back from Death's door with milk in a pipette. Then her last gasping would come to mind, and the tears would start again.

THE SMALL, yellow coffin slid into the furnace. Immediately the metal doors slid shut. A curtain was drawn across them. The mourners trooped out of the chapel. Then they trooped back. The curtain was opened. The metal doors slid apart. Out of the fire came the coffin.

It was a film in reverse. As the days passed, Harry's mind kept returning to this incident, to incidents prior to it, and also to subsequent incidents. In this hotel room or that he would sit down on a bed. The order of events had become jumbled, and now the reiterated memories attached themselves to a mental roundabout which kept going round in his brain.

Sometimes he seemed to be riding the roundabout; a participant in its incidents, and then sometimes he felt like a man walking on a roundabout, lurching between its grotesque creatures as they loomed towards him, rising and subsiding on their poles.

Then, at other times, all the events would seem very far away from him, as if he were standing at some distance, observing things through the wrong end of a telescope. When his memories were experienced this way, he would sometimes glimpse himself – a small figure lasting out his ride, or walking between the revolving figures.

In the latter mood, it was all definitely over, but in the former everything was re-lived, as if it were the present. It was generally during the day that he could see the events with a sense of perspective – that is, through the wrong end of the telescope – while the sensation of it all happening in the present usually came upon him during the night, after he'd been smoking, or as he began to surface from his sleep at some late hour of the morning.

Near or far, large or small, images kept re-appearing in his mind's eye, prompting reminders of times and places: the walk in Kew Gardens, the desert trip, the day before Dawn died. There was a horror in this, and an incongruity about the juxtapositions experienced when the images got thrown against each other by almost simultaneous recall. Now he was growling at Dawn like a tiger. Now he was nuzzling Rosemary in the dark. Next he was swaying on top of a camel. Inge's finger snapped. And within an hour most of their friends were with them. Now they were skiing at Plancher-des-Vaches, a lovely small hotel in Val d'Isère. That night, at his mother's farm, Dawn was quite violently sick.

8

THE CONGRESS is not a genuine literary event. That much becomes obvious on the day of its inauguration. At this, all the delegates are obliged to shake hands with the president and his lady: first the Soviets, then the Egyptians and the Libyans, then the PLO and the one or two black writers who have been invited to give papers, and finally the observer-delegates, including Noriko and Harry. Three of the opening eight speeches are given by Philippine generals. These are harangues read from the scripts in halting voices, for the most part equating culture with national identity and discipline in the streets. The speech by Marcos himself is slightly better contrived – it includes references to education and greater understanding between nations. It is given in Tagalog and translated into English and Russian after every phrase by a brace of interpreters. Many of these opening speeches are dealt with in this manner. There is a simultaneous translation system, but for some reason this is not working efficiently. Many of the speeches given during the other sessions have to be delivered in triplicate this way, though the Arab delegates appear to be having no difficulty with their headphones – which is fortunate, for otherwise the whole business would take even longer. As it is, everything takes a very long time to say, and consequently, after the initial papers have been read, there is never any time left for debate. Not that anyone in his right mind would care to voice an opinion. Speaker after speaker rises and launches forth in the remorseless jargon of propaganda. This is invariably Marxist in tone, which is surprising, given the absolute capitalism of the host regime. But then the congress has been largely sponsored by the Russians.

Harry spends most of his time in the bar. Or he swims in the generously proportioned pool which occupies the central courtyard of their hotel. The pool is always empty, though sometimes one of the pretty brown students will sit in a deck-chair beside it while he swims.

Perched on a bar-stool, or sprawled on one of the sofas in the lobby, Harry often chats with Hernando, the suave, tall Don Juan of a man, who writes the president's speeches. It's difficult to equate this dictatorship with such a charming fellow – for Hernando possesses charm without appearing unctuous, although he is certainly smooth.

'Ah,' he sighs. 'If I were not so continuously employed, I would sit down to write the definitive novel of the Philippines.'

'That would be some task. It strikes me, Hernando, that the Philippines epitomise diversity. I haven't toured around, but I imagine each island to be different.'

'That is the case, my friend. Every island has its own identity: there are communist islands and Muslim islands, and then there are the racially-mixed islands –'

'And the magic islands and the floating islands and the desert islands.'

They laugh.

'But if I were writing a book about the Philippines,'

says Harry. 'I would want it to be a very dry book. The Philippines seem so lush. It would be all too easy to write some torrid, South Seas romance. But I'd say you'd want to offset that moist, tropical lushness. From what I've seen, Laclos should provide the model: a dry analysis of relationships engaged in particular intrigues.'

'Yes, I see what you mean. And I know that our poets all too often suffer from too elaborate and decorous a style. You would think they had all modelled themselves on Dame Edith Sitwell.'

'Oh, no, none of that. A dry book is what's needed.'

'Something with a hidden edge, but sharp, sharp all the same. I think this is a question of finesse; knowing how to underplay the hand.'

They tip their glasses towards their lips, then Harry puts his down. Folding his arms, he looks straight at his friend.

'Hernando, you're intelligent. Obviously you can write. Even in translation I can tell. Why do you hang around?'

'Well, Harry, observe, I'm not saying I particularly like what I am doing. Yes, I have talked with Garcia. He is a pretty cool guy. He reckons I should just be a writer and cut this political junk. But you know, Harry, I do very well out of it here. And now I've developed tastes, don't you see, which are, shall we say, expensive?'

'Bet you have, Hernando. But tell me, what happens next? When this little lot goes under, do you go down with the ship?'

'Ah, there is that risk, I am afraid. But then, Harry, I do have a beautiful salary, and a beautiful family – and a very beautiful mistress. What can I do? Unfortunately this deal is so remunerative. And you know, I have influence. And also I have a very special *rapport* with Imelda. My inamorata is very close to her, my friend. And the First Lady, hell, I can tell you, she's just about as powerful as the old man. Maybe not quite so powerful, not in the final analysis, if it ever came to that. But she sure is a very powerful person here. Each of her ladies is from the elite, you see. So right now, Harry, through the elaborate machinations of desire, I get the ear of Imelda. While through my efforts on the literary side I get the ear of the boss.'

'OK, but what are your speeches? Do you think they're literature? Come on, Hernando. You've a nice style, I grant you – a little flowery maybe, but that goes for all you, here in the Philippines. Yes, but you know what those speeches are?'

'Crap. My speeches are crap. I know. Sure, I'm aware what they are. And you happen to know it too because you're the real thing yourself. But just how much do *you* make a year? How much do you make?'

'Writing like you do though, Hernando. Look, it's bad for your style. I guess it makes it all the more flowery. Now the Philippines doesn't need flowers. In flowers I was smothered when I first arrived. What it needs is dry – a cutting edge – that's what you just said.'

'That's what Garcia said too. Not in quite the same words. But he said it was bad for my style, this political junk. And yet it is a discipline, my friend. To write what you don't believe at all with total and utter conviction. Once you can do that now, it has to mean that you're getting somewhere at least. Besides, Harry, besides . . . '

'Besides what, Hernando?'

'Besides, there's another thing.'

'And what's that?'

'Harry, the aura of power.'

'The what?'

'The aura of power.'

'You have got to be joking.'

Hernando toys with his drink. 'My friend, power has a certain fascination. It has a karma about it. Maybe it's bad – but it sure is a strong emanation. And just you look at me. I'm not sitting in some garret. *I* have my own government department. I'm right at the hub of things here. Let me freshen your glass.'

As Hernando rises, a beautiful brown young girl comes over. She flashes a smile at the script-writer and then sits down on the sofa next to Harry.

'I've been recruited by Miranda Cruz,' she says, taking his arm as she leans over and looks up at his face. 'I'm supposed to look after you guys. But, boy, are those Soviets a dull bunch. So I've come over to you. I like you most, Mr Harry. You seem like the genuine article, as they say.'

It could be said that there's something genuine about Harry, or at least about his writing. He's not merely an official writer sent to the congress by the state.

INGE AND I could hear the festivities long before we reached the village. The camels cleared their throats. Their ears twitched as they dipped the prows of their necks with each step plodded forwards. A faint, high-pitched, trilling sound could just be heard in the distance.

But at that late stage of our trip neither of us were paying much attention to our surroundings. We were both numb from the night. My own mind had gone on ahead. We would take the bus out of the village the following morning. The next night would be spent in Marrakesh, and the next day we would be back in England. By then it would be important to have an attitude prepared; an attitude to the past, an attitude to the future.

Where was our marriage going? This was for our friends to judge. Our friends resembled jurors. I needed to work out my defence. Of what did I stand accused? I stood accused of sex.

I stood accused, and now I would have to agree. Sex was my stumbling block. It was sex which had screwed up my life. Sex had let me down.

All of us had problems − even our non-throw-away friends. One had a problem with drink, another had a writer's block, a third was schizophrenic. Someone else hid away his paintings because he had a terrific chip on his shoulder about 'the art-world'. There was a woman who couldn't eat, and a girl with no confidence whatsoever. Several people had too many babies.

My problem had always been sex, ever since the first time I'd got caught in the bushes with the son or daughter of a neighbour at some early age. The difficulty was, I could never see sex as wrong, or at any rate wrong for me, any more than the man who drank could believe that booze was the evil where he was concerned. And the friend who never wrote − it was not that he had a block, it was just that there was nothing left to say. It stood to reason that the madman never doubted his own sanity. And as far as the man who hid his paintings was concerned, the art-world was indeed corrupt. The anorexic girl hated food; and the girl with no confidence thought that her work was poor. The people with large families simply adored having babies.

I could see no harm in my own failing. To me it was not a failing, it was a predilection. If something gave pleasure it had to be good. That was my philosophy. And so I pursued pleasure, even when it led me straight to the Vale of Tears.

And what was Inge's failing? I turned around as far as I could in the high, wooden saddle. Inge was some distance behind now, completely withdrawn into herself. She made no effort to make her camel catch up. The strange trilling sound ahead was almost like a wail.

Inge's problem was her haughtiness, or it had been before. She was tall, and she was handsome, and she spoke the English she had perfected at Cambridge with a slightly nasal twang. She valued the intellect, and she valued beauty, and she valued wealth. If you were dumpy and poor she would sniff, and if you were wealthy and dumb she would frown.

She disliked me smoking because it affected my intellect. She looked down her nose at my lady friends because they were less attractive than she was. There were times when she thought I should earn more money, and she would never have married me had I not bought the house.

This at least was my notion of her as we rode back to the village on our camels. But it was not necessarily her notion of herself. I could not be cognisant of that. I was not in Inge's shoes any more than I was riding her camel.

The funeral had brought home to me how alone people were. Our friend Robert had embraced me. But how could I know what Robert actually felt? How could Robert know how I felt? Of us all, my mother seemed the most affected. She had come to us as soon as she had heard. And she had held onto me and she had cried. Then, at the funeral, my own feelings had somehow not been engaged. There was a dry sadness about the event, but I felt no anguish for Dawn. At least, I felt that I felt none. Inge's face had been pale and still. Only my mother had bitten her lip against tears. At the usher's call, we had trooped into the chapel. We had found seats and waited. After some brief words, we had stood. There had been an occasional cough, a shuffling of feet, then music on tape: the first phrase of *Jerusalem*.

Everyone sang, but somehow that jubilant hymn sounded more like a dirge. The curtain was drawn, and the steel doors opened. Some very simple mechanism activated a set of rollers. The small, yellow coffin slid into the furnace.

WE RIDE THROUGH a line of palm trees which stretches as far as the eye can see in either direction. Next we cross a wide tract of wilderness over which white stones are scattered. Noon has been and gone, and now our shadows begin to fall in front of us. The faint trilling wail is growing stronger. Perched on the hump of my camel, I begin to recognise certain landmarks I noticed as we started out: the skull of an ass, a broken house, the sign for Timbuctoo.

The low, white walls of the village can just be made out in front of us now, as distinct from the white stones which lie spread on the ground, from our shadows all the way up to the far walls themselves.

'I can see the village,' I shout back at Inge.

There is no reply.

'Inge, I can see the village.'

I twist myself around. Inge merely shrugs. It's exhaustion rather than lack of interest. She trails behind on her camel, shrunk into herself. The ululations increase. But Inge seems not to hear them. Never has she seemed more remote.

'WHY DID YOU stop? Why did you stop?'

He did not answer. Instead he zipped up his front and began to release her. The gust of a breeze shook the shutters then, and grains of sand were sent rolling across the floor.

The knots in the ties and the scarves he had used were now very tight. He wrenched at them at first, and only succeeded in making them tighter. It was with some difficulty that he finally got them loose. As he fumbled with the knots at her ankles he was very aware of her nakedness. She lifted her head to watch him.

'You didn't ejaculate, did you?'

'No.'

'So you can't even manage that?'

'No, Inge.'

'Christ, you're a shit.'

Having freed her ankles, he moved to the head of the bed and began working loose the knots at her wrists. A dog began barking in the street below. Once she was released, she sat up rubbing her wrists. Harry went and stood by the shuttered window. Inge reached for her panties and her slacks.

'Do you need to stay any longer here?' he asked. 'Personally I wouldn't mind getting back. I don't think the desert is doing much for me.'

Inge dressed in silence. He sensed her lip begin to curl.

'Inge, do you want to stay?'

Inge shook her head.

THERE WERE SOME beautiful brown young boys recruited as well as the girls. The celebrated old poet seemed especially pleased to have them as his escorts. The boys loved to laugh and whisper naughty things. They often came and sat with me as I sunbathed after a swim in the pool.

'Ooh, Harry, your skin is just so white. Do be careful, my dear. The sun will scorch you utterly to death. Mmm, I should like to see you totally naked. Let me feel your biceps now.'

'Cut it out, Jun. You're smothering me. I'm not that sort of a guy.'

'And what sort of a guy are you then?'

'I'm sort of bent, I suppose.'

'What do you mean by that?'

'I'm not gay, and I'm not exactly straight. That's what I mean by bent.'

I told them I would like to see a cock-fight. The two boys who were with me clasped their hands together and laughed.

'Oh, but you don't want to see that. Harry, how could you? It's so cruel, you know.'

But once I was dressed they swept me out of the hotel. Soon we were bouncing down the coastal carriageway in a brightly coloured taxi, heading for the city centre. Then we rattled along frantic avenues where neon signs got in the way of each other under webs of telegraph wires, and where the metal roller-doors had been pushed up to reveal the entrances of garage-sized shops. Life in downtown Manila went by too fast for my eyes to take it in. Our taxi weaved in and out of bicycles pulling wooden trailers piled with tropical fruits or sheets of asbestos. We dodged tricy-cle-trucks and squeezed past lorries decorated all over. The horn was sounded many times. A general nervous energy prevailed. The boys gesticulated continuously and chatted and stroked my arms.

'WE DIDN'T love her enough.'

Inge's phrase stays with him as the bus takes them to-wards the mountains and away from Marrakesh.

'We didn't love her enough.'

But how much love would they have needed? And now, is it love for her that's required? Or is it love for themselves or for each other now that she is gone? For Harry hates himself at this time. He hates himself for not having been there. He loathes his memories of the night before she died. He had not loved her enough. He had never managed to get her milk right or her nappies straight.

Inge is trying to read. But the bus jolts and lurches and

she looks up. She glances at Harry, then looks away towards the mountains.

'I can't wait to see the desert,' she says, and she turns back to him. 'Harry, shall we really get onto camels? I've never ever ridden one. Aren't they terribly high? What if one falls off?

'You get used to it,' he says. 'You get used to anything if you ride it for long enough – even a yak.'

They laugh. She turns to the window again. He watches her biting a nail.

Is this merely a sign of her apprehension concerning the beast she will have to ride? Harry wonders. If he loathes himself, he guesses that she loathes herself also. Not that she has any reason to, objectively. She was there, and at least she did what she could. He was the one out gallivanting. She has nothing to feel ashamed about. Yes, but it doesn't work that way. She carried the child in her womb. She went through labour, felt the tug of her baby's mouth on her breast. She was a mother. Feeding his leveret through the pipette was what mostly endeared that tiny creature to him. Psychologists maintain that labour pains are a bond, endearing the child to the woman who bears that child. To go through pain for someone makes that someone precious. Pain is stronger even than degradation and submission to indecency. He may not have loved his daughter enough, but Inge certainly loved her. She must have loved the creature for whom she suffered pain. So if Inge feels that her love has not been enough, it's likely that she is now experiencing a self-loathing even greater than his own. Why did she lose her milk? Why did she not get up in the night when she cried? It's all guesswork on his part. But at this juncture the likelihood of her pain seems plausible enough.

He takes her hand, which lies on the book on her lap, and he gives it a squeeze. She turns her head and smiles. Then the smile fades.

'I keep thinking of what Susan said.'

'Fuck that. There's nothing in that, Inge.'

'But it's so odd, really, how things just seemed to pile up before it happened, you know.'

'I don't see it that way. Something dreadful happens, and it throws everything into a special light, that's all. You can't start seeing the hand of fate in things. If you do, where do you end up? At séances? That can be bad.'

He has gripped her arm and is speaking close to her face. An old woman with a hen in her lap has turned round to look at them. He becomes very aware that they are the only Europeans on the bus.

Inge's face is pale. He relaxes his grip on her arm and leans back in his seat. His whole body is tense. Why does this affect him so much? Because it is all humbug. Bullshit. Just the sort of interfering, pseudo-psychological, quasi-mystical crap that gets suffering people off on the wrong track. He clenches his hands into fists and then tries hard to relax. The worst of it is you don't forget, even though you deride such remarks. He can still hear Susan's voice.

'What I want to say to you guys is that sometimes, well, you sort of get an idea something is going to happen.'

'WHAT ARE WE going to call him?'

My own name is Harry Harker, and I sit cross-legged on one of the beds in the Oriental bedroom. My wife, Inge, is sitting on the ledge which links the two beds, thus creating a horse-shoe seating arrangement around the low table covered with tiles from Isfahan. Enormous cushions are propped against the mulberry-covered walls, and Islamic embroideries have been sewn onto the cushions. Inge leans back and sips her mint tea from one of the small glasses we brought back from Turkey.

'How do you know it'll be a him?'

'I don't, I suppose. We have to have names for a girl as well.'

Inge rubs the small of her back. Her Syrian gown shows the bulge.

I tighten my lips and inhale. I then offer Inge the joint. This is a thin cylinder of pure grass made with a single paper.

IT WAS FEAR of the storm that killed her. It was fear of the storm in themselves. They would separate, and in so doing they would tear their daughter apart. They were false parents similar to the woman who contested a child before Solomon and demanded that the child be divided between herself and her rival. They would scratch each other's eyes out and snap each other's fingers off and destroy their home and destroy their child. And now Harry was flying from the storm. He was putting as many miles as possible between himself and Inge. And yet he could not return to Gertrude Stein. *Geography and Plays* lay cover-upwards in his lap. He thought of the Polaroids in his wallet.

These Polaroids were all of Inge. He had taken them at different times when the light was good, and when he remembered to take his camera with him. Now, as the cabin tilted, high over the Indian Ocean, Harry considered these. He hardly needed to get them out. Their existence in his inside pocket was all that was needed to trigger the images: Inge in her orange dress, Inge at Val d'Isère, Inge in Turkey.

His favourite was of Inge in her orange dress, which was actually red with orange ovals. A red and orange dress with a low, rather Spanish skirt part. He had met Inge in the era of the mini-skirt. She had worn one of these to an early rendezvous with him in Hyde Park. Inge was tall, and since those days she had walked with her knees ever so slightly bent, probably in order that nobody should look up her legs. However, it was some time before she gave up the mini-skirt.

Actually it was the Spanish look which allowed her to walk, stately and tall, through the Middle-Eastern bazaars; always lovely; sinuous; sometimes bumping her hip against his side.

In Iran, she had walked behind him, following swiftly through the crowds on their first day in Teheran, but then never again – her bottom had been too badly pinched. Yet unfortunately, when she walked in front of him instead, she got pinched from the front, twice as hard.

It was the bending of her knees, that ever so slight bending, which had caused the pleasant curve of her posterior; for although she was tall, she was well-rounded in that area, and much appreciated by men everywhere.

Also, she had a terrific laugh. Harry loved her in hot countries, in summertime. Then she would laugh. Then she would be sinuous and quite unlike the dour woman of the winter months. It was the Norwegian switch. She had little sense of irony. Gloomy weather made her gloomy. Hot weather brought out the orange in her.

She wore flared, faded denim jeans in London, in the winter. When she felt glum, as she so often did at that time of the year, she became somehow ashamed of her height, or so Harry guessed, and so she crouched a bit as she stood.

But this was not always the case. He carried with him one Polaroid which was a nice image of Inge during the winter months. He had taken this on a skiing trip: Inge on the slopes of Val d'Isère, in a silver anorak, flaringly reflecting the sun.

At that moment, a curve in the aircraft's flight-path brought the sun dazzling through the porthole. Harry shaded his eyes. Now he was flying away from Inge. And he realised that he had no Polaroid of Dawn. He had not been on a trip since her birth and had therefore seen no reason to keep one. Now it was too late. The hot feeling of shame swept over him, and he passed a hand over his face.

In the last few weeks there-had been few days when he had not experienced these flushes of shame and regret. He sighed. And it was with bitterness that he now mentally surveyed himself. Life had seemed so much less complex in the days when he and Inge had skied at Val d'Isère. And at an even earlier time his life had seemed gloriously simple. When he had been involved in gymnastics, he had not been required to withstand accusations or to make difficult decisions.

Then life had simply been a matter of timing. To get his run exactly right, the curve of his body perfect. And also there had been that exhilarating sense of self-control – bodily control, at any rate. He had felt completely in command of himself then, vaulting over a horse or allowing his body to fall backwards off a bar, only to turn neatly in the air and land without stumbling, on his feet.

Since he had become a writer, that sense of control had been lost. Instead an almost vicious drive kept him working at his manuscripts or sitting in front of his typewriter, and the same spirit of determination demanded fastidious correction as well as impeccable precision when it was a matter of copying out variations upon sentences according to some system – as was demanded by his abstract writing. Thus he created extraordinary texts with the surface complexities of Persian carpets, ordering words into sequences as intriguing as any in the field of modern music. Yet, except for determination, he had no self-control, or certainly none equivalent to the wonderful bodily self-control that had been his in the days of his gymnastics. And so, inexorably, life became complicated: he found himself caught in traps which had sprung up out of his own indulgencies, accused of wildness and reproached for the freedom he allowed himself.

But now he was flying away from all that, leaving behind all accusations and reproaches. He would need to buy dark glasses when he got to Manila. He was flying towards white beaches in the tropics. Already he shared a cabin with a large number of green-turbaned, tinsel-swathed people returning from a pilgrimage to Mecca. The Orient was beginning to envelop him. And now the cabin tilted again. He leaned forward and stared out of the porthole.

THE MEN positioned their cocks on the sandy floor and held them firmly but gently by their throats. Bets were still coming in from the steep, crowded tiers surrounding the pit. These were taken by men who walked around at the bottom of it. A signalling hand would be identified and the odds given on held up fingers. Hundreds of bets were taken within a minute. The crowd, their brown faces, their gestures. Jabber, jabber, jabber. It was like the *Kecak* monkey-dance on Bali. And all the time the owners preened their birds, flicked their combs or brought the two of them together so that their beaks could clash – raising the level of aggression in the cocks as well as pushing up the level of excitement in the audience. Soon the bets were taken. Then, to a roar from the crowd, the owners let go of their charges. Locked in a flurry of wings, the cocks jabbed at each other's throats.

9

'PULL YOURSELF together, boy. Pull yourself together.'

A large, red nose is practically jabbed in his face as the portly man bends over him. Large, freckled hands have him by the shoulders. They shake him, and they shake him again. His headmaster is bald and fiery. He wears a gingerbread-coloured tweed jacket. His voice is a bark, and he barks at Harry. The man is enraged by his tears. Boys should never be seen to cry.

And yet, sometimes, the tears come. If they are the result of some loss; and if the loss is felt because of love, well, the answer to that is never to love, never to love too hard, never so hard you cannot stop your sobs.

It's in the corridor of the main building, between classes. His headmaster is like a steam-engine. On the rugby field, his short legs go terribly fast, like pistons. Now he is very close to Harry, very close indeed, and his piggy eyes gleam in his bright red face. He shakes Harry and jabs him with his nose while the glances of the other boys touch him briefly as they stream past and into the classrooms, and then the head stamps off in a rage and Harry is left leaning against the corridor wall.

When he thinks about it later, from an older viewpoint, it strikes Harry that his headmaster must have overreacted. It was eight years after the war. The man had an

Austrian wife. They were Quakers. She wore white bobbles on her jersey. Harry's father had died during the war. His mother never re-married. She rented out some of her fields to the local farmers; and they brought their heifers to graze in those fields while she raised horses and dogs. She never had time to dress Harry for school.

The Austrian woman was his teacher. Presumably she had spent the war in Britain, and perhaps this had affected her nerves. Whatever the cause, she was highly-strung. She would pick on Harry and make him feel clumsy. She criticised his socks, which were forever around his ankles. She criticised his knees, which were always brown from mud or green from grass stains. She criticised his dirty nails and his unruly hair. The headmaster and his wife had no children. She had very sharp elbows and he had a very red face. They never relaxed with the boys, and they stressed tidiness and discipline. Harry was their *bête noir*.

Harry's writing looked as if it wanted to be drawing. He could not spell. There were always ink-blots on his pages, and his hands and his mouth and his ears were usually blue with ink. Twice a week, his ink-well would spill over his desk. He never ever possessed a hanky. His mother was busy with the sires of her bitches or with the mares which been to the stallion. Although she was anxious for Harry's love, her reading of books on child-psychology constrained her when she felt demonstrative. She had no wish to turn him into a namby-pamby.

Harry was never shown how to show affection. Kisses were things of duty not of desire. He never cuddled his mother. She never cuddled him. He went to school unkempt and became the butt of his teachers.

And then one night the deluded Afghan brought into the house a small, furry something for Harry to treat with practical affection. Something to nurture and cherish and stroke and be warm with. And when his leveret died, the ink blot boy arrived in school in a far worse state than was even his wont: hair uncombed, socks down, floods of rubbishy tears. 'Pull yourself together, boy. Pull yourself together.' And the head unaware he was out of control himself.

Harry stares at the ceiling. He has come up to his hotel room in order to change into swimming-trunks. But feeling tired and depressed, he has lain down on the bed.

His headmaster shook him until his bones rattled. And now Harry has stopped crying. He has stopped crying because he has stopped loving. Very sensibly, he wiped his leveret from his mind. It is Dawn who has reminded him, for the first time after years, of his games on the lawn with that small creature. It is Dawn crawling away from him under the dining-room table; Dawn crawling and turning and grinning and crawling back after him. And now Dawn is something which has to be wiped from his mind.

Is this incident from his school days why he still finds it difficult to display tenderness or show grief or feel for other people?

He can make love. He is good at it. After all, he was a farm boy with no inhibitions about his body or the bodies of others. He has always loved bodily fun – kneeling over a face or getting underneath the thighs – there are few aspects of sensual gymnastics that he has not explored. He likes to use his nose and his tongue and his fingers, and he loves every orifice of the body, all its nooks and knobs.

But now he has left Inge in London; left her wretched perhaps, in a house haunted by more than his own absence. He could tell that she was cut up by his going. He had vacillated about it at first, and she had begged him to stay. But when he finally made up his mind she closed her mind to him.

'Alright, then,' she said finally. 'You go.'

And she became haughty and withdrawn and buried herself in papers for her course. In the hours before his departure they acted towards each other as if they were strangers who just happened to live in the same house. They are both of them capable of being remote, in fact it is easy for them to be so. It comes more naturally, this aloofness, than any display of need.

But before this, Inge has begged him to stay – and has thus shown him that despite everything she needs him to be there. And yet, here he is in Manila. Harry takes a large breath, and then lets that large breath out of him.

His jacket hangs over the back of a chair beside the bed. He reaches over and takes his wallet from its inside pocket. He gets out the Polaroids and spreads them on the bed-cover before him. Inge in Turkey, Inge in her orange dress, Inge at Val d'Isère.

Harry has always enjoyed their skiing trips. These revive the gymnast in him – the gymnast of Arab-springs and flick-flacks, rather than the athlete of the bedroom. For weeks beforehand he tones-up with press-ups on a kelim. He wears ankle-weights. He stands in front of the long mirror in the red dressing-room isolating his stomach muscles.

His gymnastics career enables him to ski pretty well, and Inge of course has skied since birth in Norway. Despite the tradition of trekking which prevails there, Inge, like Harry, in confidence prefers black slalom pistes; practically vertical ones, with their icy bumps fixed like large goose-pimples to an Alp's shoulder. This she can never admit to her father who's a trekking fanatic.

Inge flares as her anorak reflects the nearby sun. In the Polaroid, her face is brown, and her goggles are raised onto her forehead. She is grinning as she squints into the camera. Skiing is another shared pleasure, as important to them as their haggling for kelims. And yet Harry has left her. She wanted him to stay, to help fill the appalling emptiness of their house. But as usual he put his career first and re-buffed her. And now she is cold and closed towards him, and he feels that she will stay cold.

He imagines her in the house, alone in London. He knows that she felt his behaviour to be beneath contempt. Why has he done this to her? Why has he done this to himself? He has thrown away their marriage for a free trip to this dull congress on the other side of the planet.

Now he raises himself up. He has left his swimming-trunks in the bathroom. Does he really want to go for a swim though? He shoves the Polaroids back in his wallet and his wallet back into the inside pocket of his jacket. But what's so special about a swim? He will lie alone by the poolside in a deck-chair. He will feel utterly cut-off behind his dark glasses. Is it worth the effort? He lies back and again stares at the ceiling.

LINES OF ululating women advanced and retreated in the white village square. They wore all their silver in their head dresses, and around their wrists and their throats they wore their gold. Now they stamped their feet as they danced. Drums clattered, and a reed pipe threaded a wavering melodic line between the drums and the dancers. Harry and Inge could hear the festivities long before they arrived at the village.

THERE IS NOTHING for it but to shrug at Inge and leave. Grass is ever greener. In the Mid-West there were girls, but there was also Inge getting our house ready as she grew larger and larger back in London. And here is Inge in London now, but there is also Rosemary, waiting for me on Mario's doorstep. One thing you can bet on, Rosemary won't wait for long. Girls are the spirits of places. I do dreamy things with them. I can be intimate with them, but they're never terribly real to me. Inge is real, her finger snaps if I bend it.

And Delphina? Is she real to me? There's an indefinable musk about her which causes me to dwell on her image. In no way can this emanation be apprehended by the nostrils. And yet it feels utterly real. It's musk of the mind, a sense I get of her worth. There's a sweetness about the long hairs on her legs, a desire to touch there, that mingles with the tenor of her intellect. She's far more than an *au pair*. She's not some jolly girl, naive from the Tyrol. Delphina won't be hurt by having an affair with me, though Inge and I might well get hurt. Or that is how I reason it.

The reality of my attraction to Delphina conflicts with Inge's reality. Inge's lovely, but she's no longer mysterious. She has great poise, and yet she agonises over what she intends to be. It's important for her to be a success at her anthropology. If she's a success, she'll like it all the more and feel all the more determined to make a go of it.

After she left school, Inge did a secretarial course in Cambridge, and then she became a personal assistant to several executives. She was good at organising paper-work and diaries, and she was soon the mainstay of some very important people. But none of this, satisfied her. Then she met me. I've only ever done what I've loved to do. Most of the time I love to write and the rest of the time I talk or I go clubbing or I make love. I've been good for her. I have no respect for mere wage-earning. I've a little money each month from my trust, and I think everybody should have a vocation. I live cheaply and know artists and writers. Inge's first husband was a painter, but he never encouraged her not to be a wage-earner, instead he depended on her wages. I may borrow money, but I've also some of my own. And I've always felt that Inge should sort out what she wants to do in life.

She gave up being a p.a., and she's tried painting. But although she loves looking at paintings, doing it herself just made her feel frustrated and incompetent. She can't bear to fail. It's part of her haughtiness that she needs to succeed in everything she attempts. One fine painting is often the product of many mistakes. Inge has no time for her mistakes. She's far too impatient to build up to a decent result by gradual stages. So as far as painting's concerned, she feels that it's really too late to start. And so she has stopped painting. What should she do? The money she's saved from her days of employment won't last her forever.

'But from now on,' she says. 'I don't simply want to earn my living. I want to do something worthwhile. Something which stimulates me and which takes me somewhere.'

We travel. We see gypsies in Kurdistan and mosques in Isfahan. We visit caves in Cappadocia and the remains of Troy. We drive down to Baalbek and we come back via Damascus and Aleppo.

I play the flute. We'll drive into the mountains, and there I'll sit on a stone and assemble my instrument. I spend a long time experimenting with elastic bands because there are always keys which stick. Finally I begin to play – usually attempting jazz sambas and ballads. Inge will go for a stroll and the jazzy, pastoral sound will follow her. I'm always occupied, even though I earn little money. Inge can earn money, but when she's not earning she never knows what to do.

We buy kelims and saddlebags and tiles. I write a lot of poetry, and Inge begins to look peeved.

'You're so damn lucky,' she says. 'You know exactly what you want to do and you just go ahead and do it. I must find something that engrosses me as much as your writing engrosses you.'

'Well, if you don't want to become an artist, how about becoming an archaeologist? You would travel a lot and get to handle some lovely things.'

'Oh I don't want to spend my days grubbing around in the dirt. And I'm not interested in the past really.'

Inge is very good at languages, and her friend Susan suggests she try anthropology. So Inge takes the relevant exams and begins seriously studying. Anthropology is very popular in her women's group.

Inge is real. She is engrossed in herself, just as I am engrossed in myself. But in no way is she merely a dream. Not now I've watched her give birth. I've seen her sweat as she pushed our baby out.

Most of the others are dreams with bodies. Even Delphina is a dream, I realise, with her widening brown eyes and her lean face and her slim waist and her rather hairy legs. Delphina is very much a dream. I want to touch her, but we've never touched. Our intimacy has only been verbal, and even then no fondness for each other has been expressed. We've only been keen on our talks.

Just as I rise to go, after having played the tiger with Dawn under the table, Delphina comes down the stairs. I nod to her and turn away. I feel rather a fool to have done a bunk from the house while she occupies the guest-room.

Delphina is a dream. But when I'm near her I sense myself in the presence of a possible reality, and hers is a reality that might be able to hold me. For this reason, she's a threat. Her knowledge about art, her swift grasp of ideas, her own incisive observations; these all work on me with as strong a magnetism as the dream of her body. She's not as handsome as Inge. But at this time, because I've not touched her and because she occupies the guest-room, she seems very attractive. I just can't cope with this attraction.

And so I shrug at Inge and leave, and as I slam the door I can feel Inge's withering contempt. I'm off to my soft options and my stash of grass, off to some dream with a body. For in some room, one of these dreams is always waiting, and so I've always had a reason for being somewhere else. This is even the case on my return from Imelda's villa. When I get back to my hotel room in Manila I find a girl waiting for me there.

ROSEMARY WRAPPED her legs around my back. Her breath came in gasps.

THEN HE PUT UP his collar and crossed the street to the car. The banality of it all appalled him; the bald facts of it: notices in the paper, death grants. At least there had not been an inquest.

He drove home. Inge's parents had just arrived. There were formal embraces. It was difficult to make conversation. Harry's relationship with his 'in-laws' had been strained at the best of times. Now it was important that Inge and Harry should get their support, and this was certainly given. But long faces were *de rigueur*. It was obviously not a time for light remarks or for jokes. Meanwhile her parents had to be offered hospitality. These were solemn hours – and they were also dull.

Death had a deadening effect. It numbed Inge and Harry, and for some months afterwards it robbed Harry of sensibility. His mother-in-law kept saying, 'This is a dreadful thing.' She did not speak English very well, and Harry had the sensation that she had learnt the phrase from a book prior to arrival. Not that the sentiment was insincere. It was just that the expression was wooden.

There was a gulf between what one felt one was expected to feel and what one actually felt. Harry's principal sensation was of bewilderment. It worried him greatly that he did not feel for Dawn the terrible grief he had felt when his leveret died. Had he loved his daughter less than the leveret?

The truth was that Harry had only just begun to love his daughter. He had obviously not given birth to her, and although he had watched her being born there was none of the nurture-bonding he had experienced when he had fed his leveret through the pipette, or rather there was some of the nurturing – but it became a chore instead of a bond.

He remembered Inge talking about a certain tribe whose menfolk were treated as if it were they who gave birth. As a woman went into labour, her man would be surrounded by helpers. He would enact the contractions with a great display of agony. Meanwhile the pregnant woman would slip away quietly into the jungle to have her child.

Knowledge of this custom scandalised the women's group – who saw it as another example of the overweening arrogance of the male. But when Harry lost his daughter, he felt bereft of grief as well. And he wondered whether some enactment of the birth-pains would have bound him closer to his child, for at first Dawn had seemed more of a liability than an object of affection. Her head had to be supported, her bottom had to be cleaned; she had to be fed and she had to be belched and she had to be pushed around in her pram for doses of fresh air.

Although he was a country boy, the stark reality of his infant proved disconcerting. There was something Victorian in his own make-up that wished to envisage women only as dream bodies. The anus was a rosebud, and the vulva was a cushion made for love. The thought of periods, or of women shitting, he kept very much in the background although it was not exactly pushed into his unconscious.

It had been decided that Inge and Harry were to share every aspect of her upbringing. This was very much the doctrine of the women's group, and in theory Harry agreed to this arrangement. In fact he found her infancy a strain. Her small body confronted him with an image of woman that interfered with his dreams. Here was the vulva – it was something that pissed and that suffered from sores and rashes. Here was the anus – it shat. As he changed her nappies he sometimes felt as if an important mystery were being violated. In order to remain attracted to women he needed to preserve that mystery.

He tried to cope and he failed, and he fled the home and tried to survive in his dreams. It was only as Dawn started to play with him that a spark of affection was kindled. She scrambled away in her romper-suit and turned and gave him a look, and at that moment she became a flirt in miniature – he could see her as his leveret, his pet. But the spark was kindled only hours before her life was snuffed out.

He was confused before she died, and her death only compounded his confusion. In reaction, he became cynical for a while. He shut himself off from feeling. Only his career mattered. Love was only fucking. He flew to Manila.

Beautiful young maidens threw garlands over his shoulders, and he accepted these with a tight, sceptical smile. He greeted Miranda Cruz and was waved through the customs into the society of a dictatorship. The door slammed. Harry adjusted the garlands and settled back. His friend from the university sat beside him as one of the Marcos's aides drove them away from the airport in the car.

THEIR CAMELS kneel in the street. Inge and Harry dismount and shake hands with their guide. The ululations and the hammering drums flood over them from the square. But Inge is looking pale. They move stiffly, slowly, in the direction of the hotel. Children dash past them, and then some hooded men in blue robes go by. The celebrations continue to rise towards a crescendo.

'I'm too tired,' says Inge.

'What?' says Harry. He has turned to watch the men in their blue robes flowing towards the square.

'I'm too tired,' says Inge again. 'I simply can't take it in.'

Harry pushes open the door of their hotel.

'WELL IT DOES, Harry, it just does. You don't seem to relate somehow. It's like you're not there. You become self-engrossed, completely self-engrossed. And you become repetitive too. I wish you wouldn't do it.'

'You used not to mind. You used to do it yourself.'

' I don't do it now.'

'You don't do anything now. You won't come to see Steve. You don't want to meet Rosemary.'

'Why should I have to? I think all that sort of thing is

rather silly anyway. I wish you could grow up.'

'What do you mean, grow up? If growing up puts an end to things, I don't want to grow up.'

'That's escapism, really. Doing these silly things just puts you in a state of mind you should have left behind.'

'You used to like doing them. We used to have fun, Inge.'

'It wouldn't be fun anymore. And I don't like being pushed. That's what makes me resist you, Harry. I don't like being pushed.'

'But you're pushing me to stop.'

'You're pushing me at her.'

'The trouble with you is you have grown up. You did it when Dawn was born.'

'Maybe I did.'

'I think it's a shame.'

'Look, Harry, I want to get somewhere. I want anthropology to work for me. And with Dawn to look after as well I haven't time for things like that. I simply haven't time.'

Inge goes off to her course, and I am left with Dawn. Delphina has gone to see the Wallace Collection. Luckily Dawn is asleep.

I go to my room and try to write, but all I can think about is Inge and what she's just said. Perhaps giving birth makes you grow up. And yet Inge hasn't lost her sense of adventure.

One bright summer's day, we drove out to a nudist colony in Borehamwood. Inge was very dubious about it at first; but after giggling a bit we went out flushed and naked, into the pinewoods, me with Dawn on my shoulders.

People camped there or stayed in chalets. Young sun-bronzed couples said hello to us as we passed. They were not terribly sun-bronzed – it was England, after all – but nevertheless there were no white patches on their bodies. Instead they were lightly tanned all over. Lizard-skinned veterans of the colony sunbathed in deck-chairs, and housewives wearing nothing but flip-flops queued outside the little shop.

It's peculiar to sit in a quite ordinary café with nothing on. The plastic seats feel strange against one's bare buttocks. Even our Cornish Pasties tasted unusual, I remember. At that time, Inge had not lost all her milk. It was lovely to watch her giving Dawn her breast, naked among other naked people.

We went outside and sat on a grassy bank. Below us, fathers threw Frisbees for their children.

'Actually it's very nice. It's so relaxed,' said Inge. Dawn gurgled on the blanket beside her. A beautiful girl walked by with her arm around her man. The girl's pubic hair was a thick, sandy bush. Her breasts swung, and the man's penis joggled a bit as he walked along. The frisbees floated through the air, and naked boys raced to pick them up.

Later a slight chill in the air began to give us goose-pimples. Inge put on her woolly jumper, but otherwise she remained in the nude, while I sprawled like a God. I admired the ripe curve of Inge's bottom. I felt part of her, as if we were both in a drawing by Picasso.

At length we got dressed and drove home. Inge fed Dawn, and I gave her a bath. She smiled at me as I dried her and sucked hard at my knuckles. Inge kissed her ear. Dawn fell fast asleep as soon as we had put her in her cot. Then Inge and I made love in a very passionate but still tender way. Both of us were excited by the images of the day, and by the nice sense of scandal about ourselves and about walking naked before the eyes of strangers.

And yet Inge has grown up. She has always possessed poise, but now that poise has become a stiffness. She's become very strict with herself. She works hard at the questions that are set her by her tutor. She never wants to smoke, and she doesn't like me smoking, and she definitely doesn't want to see Steve or do anything with Rosemary. Her term is well under way. All she wants to do is to concentrate on her course and then eventually go either to Oxford or Cambridge – but this time not as a mere nobody enrolled on a secretarial course.

But me, I remain Peter Pan. I still live for adventure. Life should always be a matter of play rather than work; and the best work comes out of play – although you then have to work very hard at it. Anyway, that's how I feel. I shall go on thinking of myself as a boy, and I resent Inge's new, grown up attitude.

There's nobody I can talk to about this – not among my serious artist friends at any rate. I'd like to go on having adventures, but contrary to popular belief, artists are generally very respectable, and you're much more likely to find swingers among dentists and chartered accountants – I suppose because these professional types are more interchangeable than artists, or so artists would have you believe. So there's no one who feels like I do about having adventures among the friends who are not throw-away people. These artists are all frightfully monogamous – they've sown their random oats while at art-school, and are now busily proving that they're just like ordinary people. So intensely do they care about this that they become more ordinary than anyone else – at least this is true for the straight ones. Some of the gay ones are different, although most of them are involved in some long-term relationship, just like the straights.

Where has Bohemia gone? Wherever it is, it's not in "Swinging London", and it's certainly not the stamping-ground for London's artistic *milieu*.

But why am I still a Bohemian? I don't know. I've been one ever since I was eight years old. I've always gone off into the bushes with people, or met them in the drying-room, or gone back with them to their flats. I don't want some one-track-minded monogamy. Making love is basically the one way I make contact, and it satisfies my curiosity, and maybe one day it'll give me a trunk, just like the little elephant with the insatiable curiosity.

A few days after our disagreement about Rosemary and dope-smoking I wake up with an erection. Inge is already up and dressed. I go downstairs, wrapped in my towel. My erection shows beneath it. I try to get Inge to come back to bed. Inge refuses. She's feeding Dawn from the bottle. I want to hold Dawn. Inge doesn't want me to. I grab Dawn's arm. Inge won't let go of her. A fight starts with Dawn in the middle of it. My towel falls to the floor as I use both hands to pull Dawn away from Inge. Delphina comes downstairs to find me naked, struggling with Inge over Dawn. Dawn starts to wail. This fight starts between the dining-room and the kitchen. Many of our fights have started here. It's a violent spot. Delphina tries to separate me from Dawn and Inge. I tell everyone to get fucked. I run upstairs and get dressed, then storm out of the house. I go to see Mario who tells me that he's off to New York for a few weeks. While Mario's away, I stay in the Never-Never Land of his flat. I bring Rosemary there, and I smoke grass there. One afternoon I visit Dawn, Inge and Delphina. I play the tiger with Dawn, then I rise to go. Inge seems calmer. I like my house and my daughter, but I need a little more time in an independent space before sharing my life with my family again. And so I shrug at Inge and leave. I go to Mario's flat and get in touch with Rosemary and Tom. The night after my visit to the house we meet at a party.

A BELL JANGLED as he closed the door. Harry explained what he wanted.

'And how much do you wish to pay, sir? Prices vary depending on the wood quality, and on the fittings.'

'We don't want anything elaborate. The cheapest will do. It's going to be a cremation.'

'Then the ordinary pinewood variety would be sufficient. Have you applied for a death-grant?'

'Yes, we have.'

'And where is the deceased now?'

'She's still at the hospital. I think they're doing a post-mortem.'

'Yes, sir. Now which hospital would that be?'

'It's the one just up the road, towards Highgate.'

'New End?'

'Yes, that's right.'

'And where is the service to be, sir?'

'At Golders Green, on Tuesday.'

'Golders Green on Tuesday. And what is the name?'

'My name?'

'I will take your name, sir. But what I was after was the name of the deceased.'

'I see. Well, her name. It was Dawn, Dawn Harker.'

'And your own name?'

'Harold Harker.'

'And may I have the name of your wife?'

'Inge, Inge Harker-Sund.'

'And at what time is the funeral?'

'Two o'clock, I believe.'

'Very well, then. We can take care of everything from here, sir.'

'Fine.'

'What is your address?'

Harry gave their address. At last the details were complete. He nodded goodbye, reached for the handle of the door. Again the bell jangled. Then he put up his collar and crossed the street to the car.

IT WAS A THIN cylinder of pure grass made with a single paper. I inhaled deeply and held my breath. I looked at the back of my hand and could see every line in my skin, every pore, the glint of each miniscule hair. I let out my breath, taking the last of the smoke into my nostrils. Then I inhaled again.

The pocket trumpet chortled at the edge of the drum; a thin, fluttering, flickering line of sound. Then, out of desert silence, the ankle-bells began their rhythmic stamp. Music of faraway places, places with little in them: drifting dunes or plains, bisected by a single track.

I took up my pen. It was good to start writing before inhaling the last of the joint, which now lay in the ash-tray, two thirds finished, but very gently stubbed out so that I could relight it again after having written a few sentences.

Just then, I was collaging my own notes. The result might suggest sense, or be derived from notes which made sense; but the sense had still to be distorted according to some formal principle. It was only thus that I could get my work to hover between abstraction and narrative.

The surface was as important to me as the sense; indeed, the surface was the sense. The turns and twists of its syntax constituted meaning. I was after the reality of words.

Now I paused and picked up the joint. I lit it again and inhaled. The room seemed to have grown colder, and the balance sounded wrong on the stereo. I got up to adjust the levels but walked over to the bookshelf. Hans Bellmer's doll inserted her arm into another part of her anatomy. How about collaging an erotic text? Readers' letters mixed together, as if they were coupling. Wow. I began to pace the room.

When I was high, I tended to experience instantaneous, intense concentration upon whatever came to hand. The next instant, something else would come to hand, and I would concentrate intensely upon that. Then I would get interrupted and express intense anger at being interrupted although I'd been interrupting myself ever since I got stoned.

This time, as I was pacing, Inge interrupted me. She was wearing her long, fur-trimmed coat.

'I have to go into college now. I've left Dawn in her baby-cage. But do play with her a bit. She can't be left on her own all day. And then there's her bottle, don't forget.'

At this I clenched my fists.

'Can't you see I'm working?'

'You seem to be pacing up and down.'

'I'm just thinking about the next bit.'

'You still have to see to Dawn.'

'I glared at her and said, 'I'm going out.'

'WHAT IS WRONG with you, boy?'

The large, red face of his headmaster looms above him and then comes in still closer as the stout man bends over.

'Come along, now. What is wrong with you? Speak up.'

'My lev . . . My leveret.'

'What do you mean, your leveret? Pull yourself together, boy. Pull yourself together.'

IF SHE HAS not already fallen asleep, Dawn will cry when I try to put her down. Then I will have to pick her up again and continue dancing. Most of the time, we dance to reggae music, especially to rock-steady. Dawn will rest her blond head on my shoulder, and I'll support her back and her seat. We rock steady, steady to the rhythm. We dance to Julian and the Chosen Few with the Gaytones, to Bob Marley and the Wailers, to Greyhound, to Dandy, to Delroy Wilson, to U Roy and Desmond Dekker. If her mother's here, Dawn will smile at her over my shoulder as she and her father dance.

Sometimes we dance and dance, but Dawn still cries when I try to put her down. Then a walk is in order – but not in the pram. A man looks so ridiculous with a pram in the high street. Usually I wear Dawn strapped to my chest in a sort of sling or papoose.

There has been some discussion in anthropological circles about the effect of these slings. Studies of the American Indians who wear their children strapped to their backs as they work in the maize fields, have shown that children reared this way tend to be aloof and undemonstrative. Quite how it's been shown has never been divulged. Anyway, it's now considered better for the baby if the papoose is strapped to the front of the person. This way you can be sure that your child will grow up into a cuddly, warm individual. Fathers like me go striding off down the street, wearing their offspring lumpishly pressed to their chests over their donkey jackets: an uncool, up-slung, *post hoc* form of masculine pregnancy. I feel pretty self-conscious wearing Dawn like this. More than merely labelling me, it spells out I'm a father, and a hippy father at that. Even so, it's better than the pram.

Inge goes three days a week to lectures in college. She writes papers on spears with more than two heads, on Hehe cross-cousin marriage, on Zande therapeutics and the meaning of dreams in Tikopia. She reads Levi-Strauss and Evans Pritchard. Her handwriting is easy to read with well-rounded characters, and she puts her ideas in a simple, well-rounded way. In a very short space of time, she's become popular with her tutors, and she's more or less the star of her women's group.

Dawn goes with us everywhere: to dinner parties and to dance parties; to exhibitions in warehouses and to happenings in disused dairies. She's become a sort of mascot to the private-view crowd.

Just recently, Inge's milk has dried up.

AND THEN THEY clawed at each other's throats, kicking and jerking, slashing with their spurs. After the first flurry, the white cock freed himself. He rushed, and the red cock retreated. Then the white one rose in the air to land on the red one's back. His beak sought the other bird's jugular. The red cock swivelled around and jabbed at the white one's eye. This was an accurate peck: the crowd roared from the benches. The white cock loosened his hold, fell back. And now he was pursued, leapt upon by the red cock. Claws flailed, feathers flew, and the honed spurs on their ankles gouged flesh from their sides. Almost too soon, there was no response from the white. He slumped in a heap as if asleep. The red one stood on his back and pecked his head. There were dribbles of blood in the dirt underneath him. Finally his owner stepped in and tore him out of the red cock's grip. Another roar from the crowd, and a furious argument began between the owners; the white's owner nursing his now unconscious bird in the crook of his arm, the red's owner making much show of his bird's aggressively jabbing beak and darting, beady eyes. He came close to the other man, holding his bird forward in his hands, and the red took a final killing peck at the quite defeated white. A fight started.

I SAT DOWN on the bed. Delphina sat on the other bed in the Oriental bedroom. The low, tiled table stood between us. Delphina sat hunched, her hands clenched in her lap. Her face was tight with pain.

'It is not good,' she kept saying. 'It is not good.'

I couldn't look at her.

'No, it is not good,' I agreed.

There was no approaching her now. There could be

no more magnetism and no more talk. The death lay between us like a sword.

She rose and went to her room. Other than a brief farewell later in the day, this was the last I ever saw of her. By the time I came back from Manila she had moved out.

I went and got a suitcase from the alcove under the stairs. Then I went to the red dressing-room and began taking clothes from the built-in shelves and wardrobes.

Inge was visiting Anita. I had not asked her to take me to the airport.

In the few days since our return from Morocco she had contrived to be out most of the time. Sometimes she worked at the library, sometimes she went for a coffee with one of other of her woman friends. Since I had decided I would go to Manila, she had been enquiring into the possibility of going abroad herself for an extended period of time. She needed to improve her Arabic, if Arabia was to prove the focal point of her research. Iraq was a choice open to her, and so was Egypt. She was looking into both. When she decided upon something she went at it in a very thorough way.

How distant we were from each other now. If the death had separated me from Delphina, why had it not brought Inge and me together? The death had brought no one together. On the contrary, it had isolated the persons most involved.

And yet how close we had been back in the summer, Inge and I. Inge, me and Dawn. As I packed, I thought of the happy Picasso family naked in the woods. Inge had moods and so did I. Maybe by summer she and I could find that closeness again.

Yet I sensed that this would never be. I might fool myself, imagine that the door was still ajar and that I had only to walk back into my relationship with Inge. In fact, the door was at present shut and about to shut forever.

When had it last been open? Perhaps on the bus on our way to the desert, when she had laughed about the yak. And there had been a chance later, in that hotel room in Marrakesh, when Inge had asked me to pull off her slacks.

Summer had been the last time when there had been no door, simply a way into each other. But after that I had got into the habit of making myself appear remote. Dawn had started teething. Inge's course had begun at college.

I PULL OUT of Rosemary and turn her onto her stomach. By now Tom is just sitting on the bed beside us. I go on my hands and knees between her legs. I lick her from the base of her spine all the way round underneath her, lifting her hips to facilitate this. Then I come up the bed and shove into her from behind. I bang into her, kneading her buttocks as she cries out for it. I squeeze these lower cheeks, forcing her apart beneath me. And I know that were it not for my saliva she would feel dry beneath my thrusts. And because of this I thrust at her all the more savagely.

'OH, MY DEAR,' she keeps saying 'Oh, my dear.'

Harry has fallen against the radiator in the bedroom. There is at least half a bottle of scotch inside him. Inge tries to help him to his feet, but he keeps sliding back on the cork tiles to the floor.

'I don't know,' he says. 'I don't know.'

'Oh, my dear. Oh, Harry dear. I'm so sorry.'

'Is he alright?' someone shouts from downstairs.

Harry's alright. He isn't even that drunk. He simply cannot cry. And he can't pretend to cry. And pretending to be drunk seems just about the only thing he can do. After all, he is drunk; drunk enough to appear drunk. Again his feet slide away.

'I'm so sorry,' she says.

Somehow she gets him into bed. And the next day there are practical things to do. His mother arrives. She tells them what she knows.

'Nobody's sure what causes it. But you mustn't blame yourselves,' she says. Her eyes look terribly puffed.

Harry is back in control of himself by now. They talk quietly about cot-death, and then about what sort of funeral they want, and then about who should be contacted.

The police come round, commiserate and tell them that there will be no further enquiries. Harry is sent to the undertakers. He drives down to the nearest, which he has looked up in the yellow pages. It's freezing cold. He hurries inside. A bell jangles as he closes the door behind him.

INGE SHOOK her head. She arranged her body and the load she carried within it more comfortably against the embroidered cushions. Harry took another toke. He pulled the smoke in deeply and held his breath.

'I don't want a name anyone can shorten,' Inge said.

A SMALL WOMAN meets me at the end of the corridor of laughing faces. This wizened creature is Miranda Cruz, my friend from the university.

'Welcome,' she says with a monkey smile. 'Welcome to the Philippines!' She tosses a garland over my head. Now I am loaded with flowers.

'My goodness,' I say. 'Do you always do it this way?'

'Do what?'

'Meet people at airports?'

'Only VIPs,' she says archly. Her smiling students gather round. Some are darker than others.

'So this is the English poet! Oh, Randa, he is very handsome!'

They are all sinuous and lovely, with dark hair and a swing to their hips. Miranda shoos them away. She and I go swiftly through customs. Soon we are bowling along the coastal highway in a chauffeur-driven car.

'Now you must let me tell you about our wonderful congress,' says Miranda excitedly as I look out at the palms flashing past, the long American cars, the decorated trucks, the high, white buildings and the sea. 'It is co-sponsored of course by the Russians, you know, but the First Lady is hosting it here. The Africans have arrived. There are not too many of them, I'm afraid. But there is a bunch of Libyan writers, and some Egyptian journalists, and many many Russians, I can tell you. And Harry, very soon you will have the pleasure of meeting our most renowned poet, Mr Garcia Lobos; and then Noriko is coming, yes, she will arrive any minute I think, on the next plane, it could be. This is what they have let me arrange, the observer delegates, that is. Don't go out after midnight. There is a curfew, you know. And in just about three days from now we will have a pretty good reading at the fort – and you will have to wear the traditional pith-helmet and say your poems and so will Noriko. Oh, Gosh, Harry, I am so excited. So excited to see you here. I told you I could arrange it, didn't I? I told you so. I told you in Iowa City. But in the meanwhile we'll all have the Russians to listen to, and the Egyptians, and also the President himself. Tonight there's to be a reception at the palace.'

'Wow,' I say, but little more than that. I guess that I'm here simply because I happened to bump into Miranda in the Mid-West, and that it's the same for Noriko. Everyone invited will be here because they are someone's friend, or because it happens to suit some government. Tutuola will not be here, nor Evtushenko, nor Voznesenski. The congress is not a genuine literary event.

INGE PULLED my arm.

'I want to go now.'

We pushed our way out through the crowd surrounding the woman in the red bandanna.

'Let's go back to the hotel,' said Inge.

Once in the room, we lay down on our bed. All the Marrakesh street noises reached us through the shutters. A man cried his wares – though what they were we could not tell – and then a jeep shifted gears, and some reedy, wailing music floated out of a radio. Inge and I had not removed our clothes. We lay next to each other without touching. Since the day at Kew we had not been able to touch, except for the time when Inge put her arms around me in the bathroom and tried to get me up on my feet.

Now I stared at the ceiling. Small shadows walked along its edges; upside-down, above the shuttered window. Had that woman scalded her face, or had there been some trick to what she had been doing? I turned to Inge. She lay curled in her dress with her back towards me. She was not on the pill or anything. I lay back and again stared at the ceiling.

'What about now then?' That's what he'd said.

But does she want another? Does she want one any more than he does?

The red sun has sunk low in the sky, inflaming the landscape through which they move. Their shadows grow longer, extending the camels' legs to an absurd degree – they move like houses on spindly stilts, were stilted houses to move.

When they stop for the night, Inge will get a chance to practise her Arabic. It's the colloquial side that she lacks. Their guide speaks no European tongue. Inge has been trying out her Classical Arabic since they landed at Marrakesh. Nobody has yet understood her – but it's hard to tell whether this is because of her pronunciation or because everybody they meet speaks in some dialect.

Inge is still dead set on her career. Of that Harry feels certain. Perhaps she seems so keen on it because of what has happened: in which case, her career is just something to concentrate on for the moment. But Harry feels that her keenness is not merely born out of a need to find some distraction. He guesses that she wants her career as much as he wants his. Of course this is only a guess. And as a guess it may be wildly wrong. Now all his certainty evaporates. He has only his own feelings to go on, and these are to do with himself rather than her.

Deep in his heart of hearts – a phrase his grandmother used – deep in his heart of hearts Harry feels that at present he does not want a child, another child. He can't be sure that he knows that he does not want one. To know something about oneself implies certainty; the choice of definition firmly made, and the crucial decision irrevocable.

But at present he sways from side to side with the slipshod paces of his camel. Inge has fallen behind. Her own camel seems to prefer to follow the others, much to her chagrin. It irritates her considerably that she cannot lead the way or at least ride between their guide and Harry. Failing these possibilities, it would be good to keep abreast of Harry. As it is, she is always at the back.

The sun sinks lower, and the shadows of the camels' legs grow longer. Soon, surely, they must stop for the night, put up the tent and light a fire.

The decision is far from irrevocable. Perhaps, sometime, he may want another child. But at this moment in time he does not. It does seem dreadful to admit it, but Dawn's death is something of a godsend.

That one cannot think. One cannot think it. Again the unfathomable divide between that which one thinks one should feel and that which one does feel. Even this 'should', is it true? Who is to say what one should feel?

And Inge. How can he tell? She carried Dawn. She was the one who went through labour. How can he say for certain that for now at least she does not want another either?

He cannot say, and he cannot ask, how she feels. If he should ask, she is highly likely to say that she wants another. But this response is equally likely to be prompted by what she may think she should feel; prompted by what she may think he expects her to say.

Now the sun is a blood-red disk, smearing blood on the retina. It is very large, and about to touch the horizon. Their camels dip and lurch, as usual plodding onwards. Apart from the change in the light, the desert remains the same.

Well, they can just give up. Or rather he can just give up; conclude that it's all too difficult to unravel, make love without the least precaution, have another child.

But say it's the case that beneath all the conventional responses, beneath the desire to do what the other expects or appease the gods of conformity, say that beneath all this they both prefer their liberty, long to embrace this second chance to fully stretch their wings, rising again like Phoenixes, alone perhaps, but once more quite without commitments. What if this be what both of them most want, deep in their heart of hearts, deep in each separate heart?

The red sun sinks, somewhere beyond the Sahara. Now it is dusk. Their guide calls a halt. The camels wheeze as they kneel.

And that night they sleep on the hard floor of the desert under a thin blanket. Canvas robs them of stars. The camels cough outside the tent. The fire dies. It is very cold.

Inge's course has begun at college. My love-text has been accepted for publication, and I've already completed my birth-text. Now I am working on an anger-text. I am always expected to look after my daughter in her mother's absence. Inge is studying the oral sorcery of Bechuanaland. There an offended person may brood on his grievance, without uttering a curse at all. But his attitude of mind is in itself sufficient to bring harm to his enemy. In her essay, she is trying to distinguish between *Kxaba* and *Dikxaba*. She maintains the *Dikxaba* always happens after a quarrel in which one person nourishes a sore heart against their opponent. However, even if you don't intend to attack the other person, the fact that you feel anger against him is sufficient. Yet apparently *Dikxaba* is merely the plural of *Kxaba*. Why should the plural imply deliberate malice when the singular does not? Is it because in the plural word the spirits show the anger? Or has she misread the data? It's the difference between bad feelings, bad feelings between people; and a bad feeling, a bad feeling that possesses you. I wonder whether you can be affected by your own *Kxaba* – bringing down a curse upon yourself.

It's difficult to write, except when Dawn's asleep. If I leave her in her cage while awake, she'll rattle the bars and wail incessantly. When I can't stand it any longer, I rush downstairs and pick her up and hold her against my shoulder. Both hands are needed – one to support her seat and one to support the back of her head. There's no way I can write with my hands full like this; and anyhow Dawn will begin to cry if I remain still for a moment. I usually put on a record and dance with her on my shoulder until she falls asleep. Rock-steady, man, that's what she likes. But if she hasn't already fallen asleep, Dawn will cry when I try to put her down.

SHE WOULD CLIMB over the bedclothes searching for his face by stretching herself tentatively towards him with the tip of her nose quivering. Harry did not sleep with her. She was so small he might easily have rolled over during the night and crushed her. Every evening, after his bath, he would get into his pyjamas, and then he would go to his mother's room to make sure that his small companion was comfortably bedded down in her box.

In the morning he would collect her from her box and take her into his bed. Then, for some twenty minutes, before he had to get up and get dressed for school, they would play together in the bedclothes. She loved him ever so quietly stroking the fur under her throat with the back of his little finger. Whenever he stopped, she would butt at his hand with her head, her long ears flattened against her back. She liked to approach his face, test it with her whiskers, and then whiffle her nose against his cheek.

For one whole week, his mornings were a delight. It was summer. Light streamed in through the window all that week, and week-long the birds twittered under the eaves. It was very hot on the lawn, and the apples enlarged on the trees.

Then the weather changed. On the last day, increasingly dark clouds rolled across the sky. In the evening there was thunder.

In the morning there was nothing.

THE PHONE rang. It woke me where I slept, wedged rather uncomfortably between Tom and Rosemary. I leant over Rosemary and picked up the receiver.

'Harry?'

'Yes, what is it?'

'Something's happened to Dawn. Oh, Harry, come over quick. She's had a fit or something. I don't know. Oh, Harry, quick.'

'I'll be right there.'

'No don't come to the house. Come to the hospital. The hospital at New End, near Highgate. That's where we are, have you got that? Harry? Oh, my god. I think she's dead, you know.'

'I'm coming now.' I put down the phone.

Rosemary had woken up. She leaned on an arm, staring. I glanced at her, then rose from the bed.

'Something's happened. I have to go.'

'What have we done?' she said.

I I

H E NEVER knows whether he's making her milk too thick or too thin. It was just the same with Inge's hot chocolate. In Norway they stayed in a hut separate from the one occupied by her parents and his mother. Theirs was the smaller hut, built earlier in the century by Inge's grandfather. Inge explained it. During the summer there is little to do in Norway but build huts. When one hut is finished, you move a little way down the fiord and build another. Every year you add to it; an extra bedroom here, possibly a bathroom there. When there is nothing more you could possibly build, you move on down the fiord. At least it's less pretentious than building another wing to your palace, that being the custom in Germany.

They used to eat with their parents on the veranda of the larger hut. But there was a hob in their own hut, and a small fridge where they always kept a carton of milk. Before turning in, they were in the habit of making themselves mugs of hot chocolate. Ever prone to excess, Harry made his of unadulterated milk, with two teaspoons of sugar added. Inge preferred hers made half with milk and half with water. It was the precise consistency of this mixture which Harry found hard to get right.

Their hut was seldom used since her father had built the new one. There were no cobwebs because her mother had given it a very thorough cleaning before their arrival.

Nevertheless the cobwebs had been there before they were swept away. The hut had a faintly musty smell, and the lamp-bulbs threw a sickly light. Inge found, it creepy.

'My grandfather used, to come up here on his own,' she explained. 'After he died they cleared it out and found hundreds of dirty books hidden under the mattress, all of them yellow and curled. It was pathetic really. My grandmother kept him on a very tight rein, I think. I used to hate it with her. She was so religious. The poor old man had no outlets. And I think my father had a hard time too. You see, Harry, he had a brother who died when just a little baby. I think that turned my grandmother rather strange. She got deeply into God. Really, it was a mania. She was not like my other grandmother at all.'

There was a high rock from which they could dive into the fiord. The water went down very far. But although it was deep it was not very cold. Once, they drove a few miles to the estate of a rich boyfriend of a nice girlfriend of Inge's. There was a sauna on the estate, just a few yards from the edge of the fiord.

The boyfriend was away. Inge's friend invited them to share the sauna. All three of them stripped off and lay on the hot wooden slats or leaned forwards to ladle water onto the coals. When they could bear it no longer, they opened the door and ran naked to the fiord, and Harry enjoyed how the breasts of the women bounced, and how their buttocks quivered as they ran.

They slipped into the fiord. Their heat insulated them – it was almost as if they were coated in oil. Harry performed duck-dives and swam underwater, twisting between the girls like a shark. The girls laughed as he slid against their legs. Never had his limbs felt so free.

All in all, it was a brilliant summer. He and Inge cut mussels from the rocks and brought them home to be boiled and eaten with white wine. They used to sunbathe naked in a hollow they had found that was screened from the fiord and those swimming, sailing and fishing in its twinkling light by a group of close-growing pines.

Inge had turned to gold. She lay on her back and smiled, and Harry lay beside her.

'Shall we go over to Paul and Hedda's tonight?'

'You quite fancy Paul.'

'Nonsense. I'm just turned on by his pots.'

'I'm turned on by Nora's little pot.'

'I noticed you eyeing it appreciatively while we were in the sauna.'

'Do you think she trims her pubic hair?'

'No, she's neat and petite, and I'm sure it just grows that way.'

'She hasn't got nice, long, silky hairs like yours.'

'Well, thank you for the compliment. You can stroke them if you want.'

There was a long silence during which the tiniest of breezes shook the bells on the heather.

'Mmm, that's nice. It's lovely here in the sun. It's like my favourite dream, you know – when I'm in ancient Greece, somewhere up in the mountains, with sheep tinkling around, and I'm lying with only a light tunic covering me, and I've fallen asleep beside a delicious pool, and Pan comes down from the mountain.'

'I know. You've told me that before.'

'So what happens next then?' Inge shifted her legs.

'Well, he comes up very close to you. And he can see you're asleep, and can see how your breasts just dent the material of the tunic. And then, ever so gently, he lifts up the hem, and now he can see your lovely thighs, and, just a little further up, your bare slit with its silky hairs, and still you're fast asleep.'

Harry loved her knees. Ever so lightly now, he kissed them. Then he raised one of her thighs and slid up into her from below. She rolled herself against him, her body open to the sun.

'Oh, go on. It's delicious,' she said. This was when Dawn was conceived.

INGE'S MILK has dried up. It's just a few months since she gave birth to Dawn. There's been less of it every day since she started her course at college. Soon her breasts will be back to their normal size. On the days she goes out, I have to make up our daughter's midday bottle. I'm sometimes stoned when I do this. I get one or two scoops of milk-powder into the bottle while sterilizing the teat by simmering it in the saucepan, but then the phone rings. I answer it, and perhaps get into an involved conversation. Still, I have usually managed to ring off in time to remove the pan with the teat from the gas before the water boils away. But then I can't be sure how many scoops I've already put into the bottle. I never know whether I'm making her milk too thick or too thin.

EVENING FELL and deepened into night. The boy who had walked beside their camels since the last encampment collected what brushwood he could find from beneath the few stunted bushes that grew on a low knoll near where they had stopped. Their guide got a fire started and boiled up some tea. There was nothing else of sustenance but a chunk of bread baked in the sun the night before. Again tribesmen had materialised out of nowhere at dusk, and they all sat shoulder to shoulder around the fire.

Some spoke among themselves, and some did not speak. Harry remembered being told by Inge that when a man of the desert wished to be alone he simply withdrew into himself. No one would give up the fire for the sake of solitude.

Inge attempted to practice her Arabic, but perhaps they spoke some other tongue. They might have been Berbers, not Arabs. But anyway, it was obvious that they did not understand her.

'Have you noticed something?' said Harry.

'What?'

'They don't pray.'

'Oh, yes. I had noticed that.' Inge became quite animated. 'Of course the tribesmen may, since we don't see them during the day. But our guide certainly doesn't. Otherwise we should have stopped at noon.'

'I don't think any of them pray.'

'None of them prayed at sunset.'

'Ah, but we can't be sure. They only turned up at dusk.'

'I don't think any of them pray.'

'Perhaps you're right. Maybe they only pray when

they're with their families.'

'I thought you had to pray to Mecca several times a day.'

'So did I. Maybe when there's no one around to tell on them they simply give it a miss.'

'Maybe they're not Moslems.'

'They have to be Moslems. They say Aleikoom Salaam. I'm quite sure they're not Christians.'

'Maybe they're like us. They just don't pray.'

'Well, I suppose that must be the answer. They just don't pray.'

'They might be feeling self-conscious in front of us.'

'I don't think they care what we think.'

One of the tribesmen began some wailing song. There was utter darkness except for the red firelight. Only cheekbones were visible, ruddy from its glow. The wood blazed away, and the fire rapidly grew smaller. Now they could feel the desert's chill on their backs.

'Let's go to bed,' said Inge.

The ground was hard, and the night was bitterly cold. Some hours later, their guide came into the tent for warmth, and he was followed by a tribesman and the boy. Not that there was any warmth in the tent. Inge clung to Harry. Harry found it impossible to sleep with her arm across his chest, her thigh across his pelvis. He had always found it difficult to sleep in an embrace – even in the most comfortable of beds. A sort of panic gripped him. He found it difficult to breathe.

This panic often affected him after coitus. It was a fear of proximity, a paradoxical state of mind usually triggered by the release of his seed. It was paradoxical in the sense that it was a feeling that usually flooded him in the aftermath of some energetic attempt to become one with another person. From an intense desire for union he recoiled into fear; the same fear as that which seized Hermaphroditus when he found that he could not escape from the clutches of Salmacis in her pool.

Hermaphroditus dived into that pool a man – he emerged from it neither man nor woman; a being utterly merged with the nymph who inhabited the water. As soon as he had spent himself, Harry would often experience the same fear of emasculation. It was as if the weight of the female lying against him were a threat to his own identity.

But out there, in the desert, there had been no love-making. It was after all far too cold to undress. Even so, the old panic came over him. Inge clung so tightly. She wanted to derive as much warmth as she could from fastening herself onto his body. Then, in that terrible cold, he felt that their identities might well solidify into a single frozen object. His panic turned into terror.

How could he breathe for both of them? He had to be Harry alone. Harry alone and on his own. He struggled to get away. But when she would not release him, he jabbed her with his elbow; jabbed her hard between the ribs. Inge grunted. Then she let him go.

Morning was slow to arrive. Before darkness lifted, Harry crawled out of the tent. The fire had burnt itself out completely. Now a faint red line delineated the horizon to the east. Otherwise little could be made out. Harry paced up and down, slapping his sides and shivering. Gradually the sky lightened. There was no bread left, and no way of making tea without spending a long time searching much farther afield for pieces of wood.

Inge emerged, her face looking pinched. Harry thought she almost looked old. He rubbed his stubble-covered jaw. He certainly felt as if he had aged. Inge went and sat on a stone; hunched over her knees, waiting for their guide. She had kept the thin blanket, and she now had it over her shoulders. Even so, she shivered all the time.

Their guide appeared, rubbing his eyes, and then the boy and a tribesman. Later, several others were to emerge. It was quite extraordinary how many people had spent the night in that small tent. Several of the tribesmen coughed, and one spat in the dirt. Then the tent was taken down. Inge and Harry did not exchange a word.

Soon they were on their way. By this time Harry had expected to have got used to the gait of his camel; but he remained stiff and sore, and still very uncomfortable in the wooden saddle. Inge was obviously in pain. She winced as animal rose finally from the ground. For the rest of the day she lagged far behind.

That day went on and on, and so did their desert journey. They rode across red ground and over stony ground. Now it grew hot. Harry removed his jumper and tied it around his waist. They rode through a line of palm trees which stretched as far as the eye could see in either direction.

THEN HE ROLLS over and puts his hand on her thigh. Inge immediately rises from the bed. She goes and stands by the shutters. They are still closed, and the room is almost dark. Marrakesh whistles and clatters below.

'I can't stand it,' she says.

'What can't you stand?' he asks, putting his feet on the floor.

'The noise, the crowds, everything.' Now she covers her eyes. 'I can't hear myself think.' Now she turns to him, shaking her head. 'I don't want to think, but when I can't it's really worse. I want to be somewhere still and quiet. Somewhere away from here.'

'Don't you want to buy things in the bazaar?'

'No, I don't want to buy things. I can't concentrate. I keep thinking I killed her.'

'You didn't kill her, Inge. I probably did.'

'I never knew that could happen.'

'Neither of us knew.'

'But I keep thinking, if I had got up when I heard her cry. '

'The doctors all say that it wouldn't have made any difference.'

'I don't care. I ought to have got up. But I was just so tired after carrying her all night at Melissa's. I was just totally tired. And I was fed up – with us, with everything, you see. So when she started to cry in the morning I really didn't want to get up. I just said, Shut up, you know. And then, when I finally went into her, it was late. I'd overslept. And by that time the central heating was on full blast. And she was just lying there with a terrible sort of grimace on her face, and going blue –'

'Stop it, Inge.'

199

'I can't stop it.'

'Inge, it was a cot-death. It was not something we knew about. Maybe I made her milk too strong.'

'We didn't love her enough.'

THE GHOST OF a cloud floated in front of a peak. It was only the faintest of vapours. Through it the summit could be seen; it was simply of a dimmer hue than the rest of this man-made sublimity. Out from beneath the vapour spilled the bush: lush, green, overpowering. I could imagine it squawking and croaking – impenetrable enmeshments of lianas, translucent, fanning palms – a night of vegetation, pierced by the meteoric arrows of its parrots.

Imagining it was as close as I got. For all this was con-siderably toned down by the time the sweep of the bush fetched up against the electrified fence surrounding the compound. Within the fence, the remaining bush had been landscaped – here was a hothouse jungle, sited outdoors for the edification of the president and his lady – a tropical interpretation of the nature-with-man philosophy.

There was not palm out of place. The jungle provided sufficient cover to screen the guest-huts from the main villa, but not enough to protect gunmen, should the com-pound come under attack. In front of the villa itself, the bush was done away with altogether, and a wide, immac-ulately mown lawn rolled away to the sea in its place. To one side of this was a dais, with a small dance-floor below it, protected by a white canopy. On the other side was a double row of stately cabbage-palms, each over a hundred feet tall; and this magnificent avenue progressed all the way round the lake-sized, rectangular swimming-pool. Steps from the poolside led down to the beach.

So the actuality of tropical bush was not to be experienced. I went for a solitary swim in the pool. Afterwards I reclined is a sort of deck-sofa, and a white jacketed waiter brought me a dry Martini. The sun blazed on the ice in my glass, and in next to no time it had melted and the glass felt warm in my hand. I realised then that my bare shoulders were beginning to smoke and hurriedly put on my shirt.

There was so much about this country which had to be left to the imagination. On arrival, I had descended into a corridor of gracefully swaying maidens and had been almost smothered in their garlands of frangipani. Then I had remembered how Christian's mutineers had been welcomed on Hawaii and had fully expected to find myself in the arms of one of these maidens by nightfall. But such a delight remained a mere figment, although it would have been a more than likely occurrence at any mundane Mid-Western university. Here they were all too Catholic perhaps – not that that had ever proved a bar to promiscuity in the Thames Valley. Here religion went deeper – or so it appeared. Either that, or they were all professional hostesses, like the Susie Wong I had met on the roof of that hotel.

Other things had to be imagined as well, like the true nature of the regime – after all, the president and his lady were so hospitable. Then there was the true state of the country. There was no way of verifying what that was. It was something one could not be sure of, like the inner thoughts of another person.

Here were a thousand or so islands. I had visited two. And then I had only been permitted a glance at one aspect of the islands I had visited. Here the green power of the bush could only be glimpsed from a distance. And in the capital they kept everything unpleasant behind a high, white fence. Miranda Cruz and I had cruised blithely past it in the car on the day of my arrival. I imagined it somehow crawling with insect life. The car swept on. Miranda chattered happily beside me. We drew up in front of a luxury hotel.

WE'RE THE FIRST to arrive. Her parents and my mother have come with us in the car. Inge has driven us here, while I've found the way with the A to Z. It's a grey morning. The chapel is built out of brick. It has no distinguishing features, since it has to cater to all sects and all denominations. Through a row of brick arches, the gardens can be seen. This is where the ashes will be strewn. We stand in a group by the chapel steps. Now, by twos and by threes, our friends appear and our relatives. We're all wearing overcoats, and people embrace through layers of insulation. We have to wait for the service before Dawn's to conclude. There's not much conversation. It is very cold.

NEVER HAS SHE seemed more remote. She's fallen so far behind that she and her camel look small, pathetically so against the waste behind them. It's strange to behold Inge like this – trailing behind, small and remote, her face shrunken, aged by her fatigue. Usually she strides on ahead. Inge likes to lead. Many of their Middle-Eastern adventures have been her idea.

It's this independent strength which he sometimes finds overwhelming. She's a tall, handsome girl, with classical features; and although he's stronger than she is, since he's wiry and fit, she's strong enough, and sometimes she makes him feel small.

Her pregnancy made him feel especially small. When he came back from America, the size of her belly disturbed him, though he experienced a strangely intense, somewhat horrified pleasure from making love to her in this state. She seemed so taut and so full; and her slit appeared distended by the weight above it. It was like making love to a lady out of a mediaeval painting. He felt he had to be so careful with her, as if she were a vase which might break. And yet there was something lascivious about it too, making love when she was big with child. He loved doing it, and at the same time it frightened him.

Her considerable strength impressed him most particularly during her labour. Dawn took a long time. Sweat broke out on Inge's forehead. The spasms came at ever shorter intervals. They happened in sets, as breakers come in sets when they roll in on a shore. The contractions might ebb away between the sets, but each set was more intense than the set before.

She was actually in labour for some eight hours. Harry had picked up an article on the subterranean workings of Disneyland – trains hurtling through tunnels at hundreds of miles per hour, computerised sewage canals etcetera – hoping that its inappropriateness might distract her from the pain. Lumbar punctures were administered, and massage – but nothing seemed to help much. For several hours she chose nevertheless to resist complaint. Finally it became too much, even for her.

'Oh, my God,' she cried. 'Shit. Somebody help me.'

He discarded the Disney article and either held her hand or massaged her. It was not an exhilarating experience. He was witnessing someone in pain, unable to help, unable to share that pain.

At last Dawn slipped into place and began to arrive. Inge vehemently strained. The doctor widened her opening with his scalpel. Dawn's head appeared between her legs. Inge pressed downward with her stomach muscles, and her baby slid into the doctor's hands.

This was an impressive performance. Inge is often impressive. It's a quality of hers which can overwhelm Harry when it's combined with her independence. Every so often, he feels useless beside her.

This is a factor which contributes to his philandering. Inge is no pushover. She takes sex when she wants it, or she has to be coaxed into it with infinite subtlety; Harry's finger alighting now on her knee-cap, now on her flank, with all the delicacy of a butterfly.

Inge was always a strong girl, but the birth of her daughter has made her into a strong woman. Harry however remains a boy. What initiation is there for him, equivalent to his wife's initiation into motherhood? The unpleasant truth about the matter may be that boys like Harry need to kill before they can become men, but killing's hardly a possibility in Harry's cultivated modern world.

So Harry remains a boy, though his wife has become a woman. Harry still wants to play, while his wife has moved on to more grown-up pursuits. Inge has no time for adventures anymore. She hates Harry smoking. In fact she's working hard at her course and has become rather set in her ways.

Other females are more malleable. When he first goes with Rosemary, she asks him back to her flat. He waits in the light of the hall while she puts a match to the candles in their wax encrusted bottles. Then they stand by the bed. Harry puts his hands beneath her dress. She moves her belly against him and nibbles at his lips. He slides his hands up her thighs to discover that she wears no panties. Immediately he develops an erection. He peels her dress right off her and pushes her back on the bed. Without ceremony, he slides into her. Rosemary wraps her legs around his back.

'THAT's bullshit.'

'It's not bullshit. You weren't living at home.'

'That's got nothing to do with it.'

'How do we know? It's like Susan says, you sort of get an idea something is going to happen. There we were breaking-up. And wanting to escape. And bang, suddenly our baby is taken away.'

'I don't believe life happens like that. I think Susan's off the wall. Things just happen. That's all. You happened not to want to sleep with me, and I happened to meet Rosemary.'

'You didn't have to sleep with her.'

'Don't let's bring that up again. Not now. Whatever happens, I don't want to see her.'

They fell silent. Inge looked at her hands. She sighed. Harry was sitting on the bed, leaning forward, his forearms on his knees. He also stared at his hands, which were pressed tightly together.

'I'd have wanted to sleep with you, if you hadn't kept getting stoned.'

'What about now then, Inge?'

Again silence. The sound of drums and car-horns came to them from the street outside.

'Inge?'

DOWNSTAIRS, in the lounge, Dawn rattled the bars of her cage. I went to her. She smiled at me when she saw me. She was standing on her own two feet in her pink romper-suit, supporting herself by the bars. Her hair was a lovely blond, and her eyes were dark and ever so slightly crossed – but that would right itself in a month or so. I reached down and lifted her out of her cage.

'Hello, sweetie. What do you want?'

I whirled her around. Then I lay down on the sofa with my arms fully stretched, suspending her above me. I pretended she was an aeroplane and then lowered her down to my face and gave her a snoozley kiss. She smelled very nice. Now I held her above me again. Dawn loved the game. It made her laugh.

My leveret had made me laugh when she crept forward over the bedclothes and whiffled her nose against my cheek.

Dawn with a sort of grimace on her face. My leveret opening and shutting her mouth.

'What is wrong with you, boy? What is wrong with you?'

The small, yellow coffin slides into the furnace.

AND THEN HER last gasping comes to mind and the tears start again. These are my last real tears. I choke on them. Then I'm shaken, and the tears stop. Tenderness is not for boys.

From now on, I become angry rather than tearful. If things go wrong, I grind my teeth and clench my fists, building up the tension within myself. Violence is the only outlet for this tension, though sometimes I go into the bushes with people, but that's not about tears, or tenderness, or anything soppy like that. That's about secrets, and seeing what they've got. It doesn't change the tension building up when things go wrong. Only a fight helps that.

I kick my mother and throw milk-bottles at my grandmother.

Later there are fights with girls.

Sitting on a bench above the cockfight, I realise that violence is to me what maternity is to women. I know that this is the stereotype for masculinity, but for me there's some truth in it. Much of what I am is modelled on this stereotype. I've always been that sort of little boy. I've enjoyed playing with guns, wrestling and pirate films.

Much of my delight in these things has been a matter of stimulus and response. You point a gun and say, Bang. The other boy falls dead. It's a sort of love dance: the world responding to me, and me responding to the world. Now I get my stimulus from sex.

I've known little girls who've enjoyed playing with dolls, but of course my best friends among girls have liked playing with guns. They've also enjoyed wrestling with me. Even so, they're allowed to kiss horses on the nose and admire their baby brothers and sisters. It's not cissy for them. But the non-cissy stereotype reserved for boys exerts a certain magnetism. In later life you can struggle to free yourself of it. But in so doing you may suppress a fair chunk of yourself.

I need to kill a few people, or at least I need to kill someone. If I'd been born into my father's generation, I might have been killed myself. Or I might have killed. Say I'd been a fighter-pilot, and say I'd survived. Then I could have returned to my wife fully initiated into the brutal mystery of manhood, and probably able to do odd jobs as well. I would have respected my wife for giving birth, and she would have respected her husband for having killed people.

But nowadays there's no one to fight – no one to fight but the wife.

The men in the pit crouch by their birds. There's some delay as the last bets are taken. Finally the pit grows hushed. A man stands with his arms raised between the opponents. Everyone leans forward. He drops his arms. The cocks are released. They fly up, colliding in the air. And then they claw at each other's breasts, kicking and jerking, slashing with their spurs.

12

H E LEANED forward to stare out of the porthole. It was in some stupefaction that he stared. The blue enormity outside was in such serene contrast to the roar of the engines, the close world in the cabin. For days, a good night's sleep had not proved available. The flight's vibrations came to him through a blur of alcohol. As well as this, at the conference, Harry had not quite shaken off his jet-lag, and he'd also found the climate debilitating. The combined effect of alcohol, jet-lag and tropical heat induced in him a strange, floating sensation, a sensation increased now by being airborne, flying on. It was as though he were slightly displaced, both in space and in time; not quite within the contours of his body, and a second or so behind the actual moment of the present.

The congress had ended, and all the delegates were being flown to Imelda's villa on Leyte, together with Imelda herself and an entourage of ladies-in-waiting and generals; an entourage which also included Miranda Cruz and Hernando. Leyte was an island somewhere – Harry was not sure where.

The congress had transformed itself into an extended party at which freedom-fighters mingled with bureaucrats, communists flirted with courtiers, and literature nodded to power or vice versa. Harry sat near the back of the plane. He was wearing mirror-glasses which he had purchased on the day before the cock-fight; the day before he had bought the small, finely-sculpted head. Once in the cabin, he had removed the jacket of his suit and had rolled up his shirt-sleeves. He still wore his tie but had undone the top button of his shirt. Next to him sat the soft, white-skinned, silvery-haired old poet, the most celebrated writer of the Philippines.

'Would you care for a drink, sir?' The stewardess bent across Garcia, in Harry's direction. She wore no jacket, and when Harry turned from the porthole in response he found himself staring down the open neck of her chemise. Harry removed his glasses and grinned appreciatively at the revealed swell of her cleavage.

'A Bloody Mary, please.' He glanced up and caught her eye; altering his grin slightly so that it came over as a quizzical smile. She half shook her head, not quite disapproving, and then moved on down the aisle. Harry craned his neck in order to see over the back of the seat in front of him, and he raised an eyebrow in acknowledgement of her nice bottom in its neat, blue skirt.

'So do you like the boys as much as you so obviously appreciate the girls?' Garcia was patting his hand.

'I like the boys,' said Harry. 'I like fondling the boys. But I'm only happy doing it when there's a girl around.'

The old man pulled a face. 'Why do you need the girl?'

'I just do. It makes me feel ok about the boy. When I was at school, I used to fondle lots of boys. But then, when I was a gymnast, I met some truly awful queens who used to sort of hang around the team. Christ, I hated that. I never wanted to have anything to do with any queen. I went right off boys then, and ever since I've never really got it on with a boy. I find it kind of embarrassing. The only way I can get it on with a boy is if there's a girl around. I love fondling a boy when I'm in a girl. That really turns me on.'

A wing dipped over jungle. The stewardess brought them their drinks. The ancient poet sighed. Then he began to stroke the younger poet's arm.

'Ah, but you have the softest skin. A girl's skin, my dear. The truth is that you are for the boys. I can tell, of course I can tell. You have the skin of a girl.'

I WAS NOT merely an official writer sent to the congress by the state. That was what most of the others were: party hacks, government spokesmen, mouthpieces for insurgent movements. Among these there was no discussion about writing but a great deal of political talk, hectoring speeches, programmatic debate.

There was one nice young novelist from Ghana, obviously serious and talented. Then there was Noriko, Garcia Lobos and myself. These were the few attending the congress who actually cared for the craft.

We were very much on the side-lines. Only rarely did we visit the reception hall where the congress proper was grinding out its dull, portentous course. Most of the time we sat in the lounge ordering Tequila Sunrises, Screwdrivers, or any other cocktail the barman could devise.

'To tell the truth, I have not the slightest idea what I am doing here,' said Obi, the black novelist.

'You are here to be polite to Madam Marcos,' Noriko suggested.

'And I'm here to see the tropics,' I said. 'I've never been to the tropics before.'

'But I maintain you writers are here as rubber-stamps,' Garcia spoke with a smile. 'You are Imelda's endorsements.'

'I don't understand how they manage it,' I went on. 'I would have thought the regime here was diametrically opposed to the PLO – yet here they are thick as thieves. And how can the communists swallow it, the curfew, I mean, and the rigged elections? Really, it beats me. Everyone gets along just fine. It's as if they were all on the same side.'

'In a sense they are, my so naive young man. They are all in positions of power. Even those of the PLO have power among their people.' Garcia Lobos scratched his thigh.

'The wife of Nasser, the journalist who got shot, she seems very nice indeed,' said Obi. 'I do not think she is a terrorist. No, not in the least.'

'You have enjoyed to dance with her,' Noriko pointed out.

'That she's Danish sort of helps their cause. It seems to lend it conviction,' I observed.

'Whether their cause is just or not is immaterial in what your C.P. Snow would call the corridors of power.' Garcia chuckled. 'You see, here in the Philippines, we wish to stay friendly with everyone. To the Japanese businessman we are a very convenient little brothel, if you don't mind my saying so, my dear.' He inclined his head apologetically towards Noriko. 'But meanwhile Marcos courts the communists. He does so despite the fact that we are the little brown brothers of the Americans. Imelda had a very great impact on China. They call her there "The Iron Butterfly". But of course the Russians must be given as many privileges as the Chinese. Marcos does deals with both of them to compensate for all the Yankee aid he has been getting ever since the war. The two communist blocs fall in upon the Philippines and get wedged against each other somewhere above us. In this day and age it is most convenient to be so friendly with one and all.'

'Good Machiavellian stuff, eh? Keeping as many people as you can as happy as possible.'

'That is correct, Harry. Our people though are treated with somewhat less civility. They must be home in their beds by nightfall. And they should only write about the beautiful flowers of the Philippines; the opalescent, undulating sea, and the special, spontaneous smiles of fishermen's wives. The rest? The rest they had better pass over in silence.'

'We have a problem like that at home.' Obi wrung a hand as if it had been burnt, 'And I once met an Ethiopian writer of short stories. Now he told me that the censors in his country would never allow him to refer to an old man. If he used the expression it had to be expunged. Never mind the text, to them such a phrase could only be a derogatory reflection on their emperor.'

'And now you're all going to turn round and point a finger at me,' I interjected. They looked round in surprise, but I went on. 'I tell you, in Iowa it happened all the time. Practically everyone from behind the Iron Curtain would point accusingly, and so would everyone from Asia and from Africa. They would all voice their complaints about censorship in their own countries. But you, they would say, pointing. You, you are the lucky one. You have no censorship in your country. You can say what you like. Some of them used to get quite angry about it. I tried to explain that there was such a thing as commercial viability. Mr Commercial Viability was our censor, I said. And if he wasn't, why was it so hard to get my abstract writing published?'

'At least you can write the stuff, Harry.' Obi said with a smile.

'I have friend from Poland,' put in Noriko. 'He write very good plays. But he not able to publish in Poland. So he – what is the word, to run away?

'Defect, you mean?'

'Yes, he defect to Chicago. He get good job in university. Now he can publish anything he want, and his plays can be perform. But the university keep him so busy – lectures, writing test for students. Busy, busy, busy. And now he have no time to write his plays any more. So he defect back to Poland. There they let him write. He very honourable professor. He get good salary just to be professor too. Only to publish is impossible. And his plays must never be perform.'

'Come on, you lot,' said Obi. 'This is all far too depressing. Isn't there a reception for us tonight? Up on a roof-top somewhere? Didn't Miranda say there was? Well, let's bloody well go there.'

We were the first to arrive.

IT'S HELL changing her nappy. This is before disposable nappies. You place the used nappy in a plastic bag. Once every few days the contents of that bag are taken out and washed. Some days the house smells of shit. Dawn kicks on her back on the table. You take a clean nappy and fold it on the baby mat. You place Dawn on a piece of wadding similar to a sanitary towel, which lies on top of the folded nappy. Then you wrap the nappy around her, knot the ends, and fix the whole lot together with a large safety-pin. This time, Harry is stoned, and he pricks Dawn on the thigh while attempting to change her. Dawn gives a sudden wail.

IN THE SPACE of half-an-hour, I meet more generals than I have seen hot dinners. They come in all shapes and sizes and exhibit as diverse a range of characteristics. Some look more like thugs: large heads, close-cropped; broken noses; large, ugly hands. Others are military dandies with silvery hair and immaculate uniforms. Then there are the intellectual ones, with gaunt faces, thin nostrils and spectacles. I suppose that these three predominant types are representative of the three main prongs of bellicose activity: tactics, drill and strategy.

There's a fourth type of general I would never have guessed was a general, were he not introduced as such. This type is dressed in civvies – usually an unassuming suit with brown shoes and a quiet tie. The face is indistinct, difficult to remember. Nobody will say what this type of general is in charge of.

There are generals responsible for protocol, and generals who control propaganda; catering generals, and generals for cultural affairs.

I've met them all on arrival at the hotel. They've shaken my hand and dismissed me from their thoughts.

But now the girls arrive, after having welcomed the very last arrival at Manila airport. Several congregate around me. I feel as if I were being mobbed by doves. They still wear their garlands over their shoulders, but the icy force of the air-conditioning to some extent dispels the sickly scent of their flowers. The girls chatter away:

'And you are from England. Oh, how exciting. Maria, come and meet the English poet.'

They're all smiles, the girls. And they sit on the sofa in the lobby with me, tossing their long, black hair and then modestly ensuring that their sarongs do not slip down. Their bare shoulders reveal their brassiere-straps.

'We do not usually dress this way, of course. Tomorrow you will see us as we are.'

'What do you mean by that? Am I to see you truly as you are?'

'Well, you will see us dressed for college – Western style, you know.'

'Oh, what a shame. I thought that you meant that you would take me to some fabulous, white, deserted beach. And that there, under the palm trees, you would step out of your sarongs, and, wreathed only in garlands, run with me into the sparkling foam.'

The girls giggle.

'Oh, you *are* a poet then. What lovely language you use.'

'But that would be to see you as you are.'

'That is not what we meant at all. Besides, there are the sharks.'

So that's as far as I get with the girls. But the next night, the entire congress goes dancing with Imelda Marcos. There's a grand supper laid on for us in the foyer of another hotel. Except for the presidential handshake, all our receptions occur at hotels and it seems likely that in some way the hoteliers are co-sponsoring this junket with the Russians. Either that, or it's an advertising campaign organised by the Philippine tourist industry, expecting us to write articles on our stay in Sunday supplements when we get home. Whatever the reason, we never enter a private house.

At this first banquet, there's a special dance the delegates are expected to perform. Two long, stout poles of bamboo are laid on the floor parallel to each other. Girls kneel at the end of these, and when the music starts they bang the poles on the floor and then bang them against each other. The dancers are meant to skip in and out, between these flashing, clashing poles. One Russian receives extremely bruised ankles and has to be helped off the dance-floor. I acquit myself with great distinction, together with a particularly agile member of the PLO. We shake hands after the bout and quit the floor to thunderous applause.

'Now that was wonderful,' says a clean-shaven Englishman who happens to be sitting opposite me at the long table. 'Where did you learn to move like that? It's most unusual to meet a writer who can move. Most of us sit on our arses all day. The niftiest part of us is our fingers.'

'I was a gymnast once. I took it very seriously indeed.'

'Really, a gymnast? I say.'

'So you're a writer too?'

'Well, in a manner of speaking. I like to get my advance before I start. I've written several guide-books on the Philippines.'

'Oh, do you live here?'

'Yes, I've lived here for years. Don't ask me how I got here in the first place. But I love it here, I must confess. Here it's so easy to be as you want to be. If you have the dosh, that is.'

On the rostrum above the dance-floor, a singer begins crooning in Tagalog. We rise from the table and go through to the hotel bar. The man introduces himself as Samson. He wears flared trousers with a crease sharper than a razor's edge and highly polished shoes. Very civil, he buys me a drink.

I'm pretty drunk by now, after the wine I've already taken on board during the meal. My tie has come adrift from my throat. I begin to confide in Samson.

'I'd like to find a girl. It seems so sad to come all this way and not to have an adventure.'

'Oh, you can find adventures here. As I say, it'll cost you a bit. But if you've got the wherewithal you just need to stick around. These days I'm more into the boys. They are just so pretty, and so easy-going. You can have the most marvellous time with them. Of course I've had my girls as well. Actually, I've had a couple of kids. They're no trouble to me at all. There aren't those responsibilities one does get so embroiled in, back in dear old *Angleterre*. Their mothers look after them totally here. I sometimes see them playing in their compounds. Not that it's easy to tell which are mine. They all look alike to me. But the boys, Harry. The boys knock spots off the women here. And they're just as accommodating, if you know what I mean. Seriously, there are some boys I could introduce you to. You wouldn't know you weren't with a girl.'

It's true that the boys are charming. Along with the girls who welcomed me at the airport, several boys have been recruited to entertain the delegates. Now a bunch of them come up to us where we perch on our bar-stools. They kiss Samson and roll their lovely eyes. One of them gently pulls at my ear.

'What shall we do about Harry, then?'

'He can come with me. I'll show him a good time.'

'You'll show him your arse, you mean.'

'And what's wrong with that? Don't I have the best arse in Manila?'

'It's not what you've got, it's the way that you get it.'

'Now, Luis, you know I like to wriggle and rub as well.'

'Ooh, yes, you love to wriggle, dear – just like a little snake.'

'Sliding into the nearest hole.'

'Just so long as the hole is at the back.'

They purse their wide, brown lips so that they go sort of purple and kiss me where they can – on the neck and on the cheeks. Samson invites us all back to his place, but it's nearly midnight. After midnight you have to stay indoors: that's when the curfew starts. I'd quite like to go on with them and have a few more drinks, but I don't want to have to spend the night there. And so I demur, as courteously as my intoxication will allow.

The singer has stopped her crooning by now, and the band is playing. The boys insist I come with them onto the dance-floor. They're all wonderful dancers. With the exception of the tactical generals, most of the Philippines I meet move with extreme grace and fluidity. Charm is abundant. Necks incline, and delicate fingers touch. But I'm too drunk to dance. Soon we shall all have to go home anyhow. I lurch back to the table. But I'm still accompanied by these male houris. The boys gesticulate continuously and chatter and stroke my arms.

'I'M GOING out.'

'Harry, you can't go out now. I have to go into college.

'I couldn't give a monkey's. I've got things to do you know, just as much as you. I haven't seen Rosemary for a week. You can't expect me to look after Dawn every bloody minute.'

'It's just three days a week, for heaven's sake.'

'I couldn't give a monkey's.'

'Have you been smoking again?'

'What on earth has that got to do with it?'

'It always makes you say that "I couldn't give a monkey's. I couldn't give a monkey's."'

'Leave off, Inge.'

'God, you're pathetic, Harry.'

'If I am I couldn't give a damn. And the reason I couldn't is you. You know what I've wanted. You only need to be reasonable.'

'What are you on about now?'

'Oh, come on, Inge. You know what I'm on about.'

'I haven't the slightest idea.'

'Of course you bloody have.'

'What do you mean?'

'I'm talking about us and her of course. You bloody know I am.'

'But I don't want to do that. Not with Rosemary at any rate.'

'Why the hell not? She's the only person I know who would.'

'I don't like her. I don't like what she stands for.'

'Why? Just because she's free enough to go with other men?'

'Well, I must say, I don't find that a particularly attractive attribute.'

'I don't believe your reluctance has anything to do with her. I just think you don't want me to do it with another girl.'

'I don't see why you have to.'

'Jesus Christ, why shouldn't I? You've had other men. What about Steve?'

'That was ages ago.'

'That doesn't matter. It still happened. Just as it did with Charlie and Jane. And we've never slept with another girl. Listen to me. Don't go away. You know I don't want to do it on my own with her. Why should I? It bores me I've got you to do that. What I want is for us to have her together. That way it's not about jealousy or secrecy or infidelity or anything. It's just a lovely exciting thing that can happen between people.'

'I don't feel that way about it.'

'Yes, but why on earth not? Why the hell not, for Christ's sake?'

'I don't want to do that sort of thing.'

'Why don't you? You always used to. With Steve and me you loved it. Why is it so different when it's us and another girl?'

'It's not that it's different. I don't want to do it now. Not with Dawn around.'

'To hell with Dawn. To hell with her. What difference does it make? She'll be asleep. Really, she's just an excuse.'

'I don't want to anyhow.'

'But why not?'

'Because you keep pushing me into it. I don't want to be pushed.'

'Oh, that's all very well. You say that, and I don't push, and then it never happens.'

NIGHT FELL again. Again they were back in their hotel in Marrakesh. It was peculiar. They had gone back to the same hotel; and then by chance they had been given the same room as they had vacated a few days earlier. Same floor, same door, same closed shutters. Marrakesh whistled and clattered below as before.

And had they changed? Had their days in the desert altered anything? That had been the idea. They had gone off to the desert in search of some metamorphosis; to undergo a change in that imagined solitude. Harry guessed that both of them had felt the same way about it, felt a similar need to change. Certainly he had hoped that in the desert some old self of his might catch fire and be consumed in the dry light there. Out of the embers of this former self, he had longed for some new self to emerge, Phoenix-like and vigorous – a self no longer haunted by the frailty of Dawn.

But this had not happened. At any rate, it had not happened to him. The desert had not meant solitude. They had never been alone there except in the sense of that solitariness which seemed to have afflicted their spirits for some time. In reality, they had travelled into the waste in the company of several presences: the presence of their guide, of the boy who had walked beside them, of the tribesmen who had materialised at dusk, and also in the presence of their camels – those wobbly, sardonic-looking brutes. The excursion had proved a test rather than a time of meditation: a test which he for one had failed.

Somebody switched on a radio down below, in the barber's across the street. Reeds wailed to a drum. Little had changed, or rather there had been a change, but this was hardly a metamorphosis, more a confirmation of their old selves, he felt; a sense of increased helplessness. They were the same, and they could not hope for a change.

Ceilings. It was a time for staring at them: the mulberry-coloured ceiling of the Oriental bedroom, the cracked whitewash of a bare hotel room in this village or that city. Here, in Marrakesh, he watched again as shadows walked upside down above the shutters. Only a few days before, they had stood talking in this room, trying to find some answer, and then lying, staring up from the bed, thinking, thinking things out. They had looked for some catalyst which might bring them closer together once more. The desert had been chosen as that catalyst.

Before their trip, he had been willing, she had not. Afterwards, she had been willing and he had not. If the desert had not proved the catalyst, at least it had had some effect. They had both changed and missed. And because they had both changed there was little difference to be found.

The shared search had turned into a private search. Harry had looked for his own talisman there, the key to his own feelings: to know them for sure seemed crucial first, before he attempted to negotiate Inge's — whatever her feelings might be. All he knew for sure was that he felt some need for a search. It had been he who had suggested the Sahara.

'We can't work anything out here.'

INGE'S FATHER is extending a summer hut's veranda. He kneels among stained wooden runners, nailing them down to a set of supporting beams. Stout timbers of differing lengths have been sunk into the slope, and these support the platform. Fifty feet below, there is the rock-strewn edge of the fiord. Between the heather's shaking bells, the water twinkles in sunlight there. Inge is inside the hut, chatting with her mother who is making lunch. In all probability they are discussing the scandal of some refugee-camp or famine thousands of miles from Norway, or, nearer to home, the table-manners of Harry's mother. The hut in which Harry and Inge are staying lies a bit further back from the fiord, a distance up the hill. On the already completed portion of the veranda, his own notorious mother is installed in a deck-chair. She breathes heavily, with her eyes closed, and her mouth has fallen apart.

Coming back from his walk along the fiord, Harry mounts some wooden steps and comes out onto the same completed part of the structure. He leans against its wooden rail, smoking a cigarette. His father-in-law pinches a nail between strong, bronzed fingers. Hammer raised, he pauses.

'Would you like to help me?'

'No, I'm afraid I have to write.'

Halvard bangs in the nail. Next, he selects a new length of wood. He lays this in place and measures the amount which needs to come off it. He saws this away, and then fits the length into place. A bee comes buzzing through the air. Harry pushes himself away from the rail. He descends the steps and strolls away up the hill. He guesses that his father-in-law is glaring at his retreating figure, before going back to hammering in his nails.

I COULD SENSE his resentment. I did not get along with my father-in law. The man seemed hewn out of wood.

I was very conscious of my own lack of a father, the war having seen to that. In order to understand what a father was, I had watched the fathers of my friends. I had no direct experience of fatherhood, and later in life I had only second-hand models of the role on which to base my own interpretation. This was another factor contributing to my Peter Pan-hood. When I thought of my father I thought of a collection of objects: my father's epaulets, snipped from his greatcoat and sent to my mother, a lizard skin belonging to a tame lizard my father had once owned, an army knife with a silver horse's head for its pommel.

Otherwise there were photos: my father bare-chested in an English field, propped on one arm, squinting into the camera, or standing with a stern young warrior look in front of his motor-bike in Naples, the bike on which he died. And my extended immaturity was also reinforced by the fact that my father had been quite young at the time of his death. I was already older than he had ever been, even before I met Inge. Yet I felt that I had to remain my father's junior.

I was a boy, not a man. I had cared for my leveret with the tenderness a boy can sometimes discover that he feels for a baby sister. Had that tenderness been allowed to develop, it might have matured into a truly protective inclination. But the chance of such a growth had been taken away from me on a dark night, just a week after the Afghan had brought her in from the fields. That night there had been the most violent storm.

'WHAT ABOUT NOW then?' I ask.

I have risen from the bed and am standing behind Inge with my hands cupping her shoulders. She remains motionless, staring at the closed shutters. A tape-recording of the muezzin can be heard, wafting down from the loudspeakers of a minaret.

'I don't know about now,' Inge replies. I can feel the swell of her rear against my pelvis, but still her crossed arms hug her waist. She hunches forward. I release her shoulders.

'Why don't we go to the desert?' I say. 'We can't work anything out here.'

13

FINALLY HE swept out of the party with Tom on one arm and Rosemary on the other. Why was he doing this? They tripped down the steps, and pretty soon the door slammed behind them. Ladbroke Grove was deserted at this late hour. Their breath steamed in the chill night air. A taxi came rattling towards them. Harry stuck out his arm. The three of them piled into the back. Harry leaned forwards towards the sliding window. He gave the cabby the address in Belsize Park. Then the cab started forwards with a jerk, and he fell back onto the back seat. Rosemary and Tom had already gone into a clinch. Why was he doing this? He felt like a theatre director. The cab rattled on. Harry was directing the theatre of his life. He was outside this. But what a great scene it would make. It was a scene from a novel or a film. His hands went under Rosemary's dress and then slid up her thighs. It was all real, and yet it was artificial too – some hypothetical scene. Rosemary pushed her buttocks against him. The rest of her was pressing up to Tom. Why was he doing this? In his mind's eye he saw Inge driving home, with Dawn fixed to the baby-seat in the back. It would have been good to have travelled home with them. But meanwhile Inge would be imagining him travelling through the night, stoned out of his brain, fondling Rosemary and Tom. Her lip would curl in contempt. She would drive a little too fast. Why was he doing this? Because he could see the scene on film, imagine it written down. It was as if he were not one of the participants. At this particular moment his life was a game. And the game had to reach its conclusion. The taxi drew up opposite his friend's flat in Belsize Park. Harry paid. The three of them tumbled out into the dark, deserted street. And now he led them across the street and up the steps to the front door. He got out the key and let them in. They leaned against each other, laughing and kissing still. Then they stumbled up the stairs. Harry had pushed Rosemary in front of him, and as she mounted the stairs he felt up her legs, beneath her woollen dress. They reached the landing at the top of the house. Why? Why had he brought them here? Christ, he was stoned and drunk.

Harry unlocked the door and ushered Rosemary and Tom into his friend's flat.

WE DROVE in a cavalcade of coaches and cars to Imelda's villa. This was a palace installed in the jungle. Its palm trees fringed the long curve of a beach. Above the beach was a very large swimming-pool, a villa, a dance-floor beneath a white canopy. As we delegates stood sipping cocktails on the shaven lawn there, Imelda briefly addressed us:

'Welcome, honoured delegates, to Leyte. Leyte is my home from home.

It is here we come when we wish for a short time to get away from the pressures of office.

Here there is privacy and peace for the President and myself, removed from the duties of the palace and the international hurly-burly of Manila city.

Sometimes we bring some work, when it has to be done, and sometimes our helpers join us and policies are discussed; but always the tossing palms and the blue sea provide us with a tranquil accompaniment to our labours.

The President felt that before you departed from our shores you should all see something of the real Philippines. That is why we have had you flown out here to an island of sunlight and greenery, far, far from the madding crowd.

Most unfortunately the President is too busy to be with us, but he has personally asked me to welcome you and hopes that you will all enjoy your stay.

And so, writers of Africa and Asia, this holiday brings your congress to a conclusion. I thank you all for making it such an exciting and informative occasion, and I thank the observer-delegates for bearing witness to this historic event.

But now it is time to relax and to enjoy the natural magic of this wonderful island.

Welcome, welcome to Leyte.'

There was more than polite applause. Imelda had been a very lovely young woman, a beauty-queen it was said, and she was still extremely handsome, with only the hint of a crease in her powerful throat. As the main bulk of the party moved over towards the drinks table, I was drawn into a chat with her by my friend the script-writer. Impassive, yet in command, there was something in her manner which reminded me of a big cat. Her fine eyes swept over me, dismissive yet amused.

'What wonderful mountains,' I said, by way of conversation, gesturing to the two high, jungle-covered hills, which rose almost vertically, one on each side of the compound.

'Yes, we had them made,' said Imelda. With a faint, unheated smile, she moved on with Hernando, leaving me to scratch my head.

I glanced up at the hills again. The dense bush of the tropics grew all over them. Perhaps they had been piled up from the earth scooped out of the compound to create the stupendous pool there.

It was into this pool, many hours later, that I flicked my Polaroids of Inge. By then it was long after midnight. The combo under the canopy had finished playing with *I did it my way*. Now they were packing up. Most of the delegates had gone to their huts.

I stood by the pool. I got out my wallet and took the Polaroids from inside it. Woozy-drunk, but sleepless from the Valium, I swayed I think on my feet. One after another, I flicked the Polaroids into the illuminated water: Inge in Turkey, Inge at Val d'Isère, Inge in her orange dress.

The Polaroids floated on the surface. I watched them for a while. Then I turned away.

In the morning the cavalcade of vehicles drew up in the compound, ready to take us back to our plane and then back to Manila. I glanced for a last time at the hills. Nothing seemed to have changed, and why should it have changed? There was nothing earth-shattering about the Afro-Asian Writers' Congress. We were just another delegation, duly given its holiday bonus. The weather had not changed at all. It was as if time had not bothered to move on Leyte since our arrival. The ghost of a cloud floated in front of a peak.

DARKNESS HAS set in. Harry runs himself a bath. Inge is downstairs, giving Dawn her bottle. Harry soaks for some twenty minutes. Then he gets out and towels himself dry in the red dressing-room. He gets dressed into party clothes: orange dungarees, a bright yellow shirt.

'Are you coming?' he asks.

'Not tonight. I want to work.'

It's Dick's party. There are publishers there, and writers. Dick has laid on a buffet: several bowls of hummus, a cheese dip, some falafels, lots of celery and quartered tomatoes and sliced cucumber, French bread and Ryvita. He's also got some wine, and everyone has brought a bottle as well. People are sitting with paper plates on their knees all the way up the first flight of stairs to the bathroom. It's crowded everywhere. In the front room, a young poet is having his head shaved by a painter wielding an electric razor. At the table in the kitchen, a large American with a hearing aid is stuffing falafels into his briefcase. If there is any music it's completely drowned by the intensity of the conversation. Myfanwy comes up to Harry while he's pouring himself a drink. She's holding a piece of celery in her hand.

'I saw your poem in *The Measured Foot*,' she says, waving her celery stick like a wand.

'Did you enjoy it?'

'I did. I loved the way you made the words come alive, as things in themselves rather than what they referred to.'

'That was what I was trying to do.'

'And I think you succeeded.'

'Thanks.'

'I think what you're trying to do is courageous. It's going against the tide of things so. I think more people should tell you, and so I decided to tell you myself.'

'That's great, Myfanwy.'

Harry likes the girl. It's not often he comes across a genuine enthusiasm for issues that he cares about. Unfortunately she's a little too respectable for him. Her skirts are always so long, and she's firmly attached to her man. They chat for a while, politely. But after she finishes her celery they nod and drift apart.

A hand fondles his bum. He turns towards a smiling, slender girl with decent breasts and reddish hair.

'I can tell that you're well-made down there: those are the firmest buttocks that I've found. What do you do for exercise?

'I used to do gymnastics. But now I'm more into sex.'

'Me as well – it's good for the figure.' She laughs.

Harry smiles. He loves girls who are forward.

'How did you meet Dick?'

'At a party. Then I took him home.'

'Are you going to take me home?'

'Yes, I think I will.'

Her name is Rosemary. She has no literary chit-chat, but she's very slender and attractive. Soon they are tasting each other's tongues in the crowded corner of the kitchen. This causes people to glance at them. Everyone knows Inge; and Rosemary is Dick's girl, at least she has been tonight – till now. Dick moves in and out of the kitchen. Harry can sense his resentment.

WE'VE MADE ourselves a secret nest in the heather above the fiord. This is after a morning of sailing to and fro across the inlet in her father's dinghy. The breeze sent us skimming across the wrinkled surface of the glittering water. Sailing is energetic work. When the boom swings, you have to fling yourself across the boat to lean out over the other side, counterbalancing the inclination of the breeze-filled triangle of canvas. We kept at it till well after lunch.

Inge and I have the huts to ourselves. Her parents have gone back to town, and my mother has returned to England. Now we relax, naked, in our nest; a small, heather-lined hollow, hidden from bathers and fishermen by firs and silver birch. Inge smiles at me. She brushes a fly from her breast. All of her is bronzed. We've sunbathed in the nude as often as we can, and now there's only a faint difference in the hue of her skin to suggest where her bikini has covered her. She's very beautiful, and tall – or rather she's long, now that she's lying down. And so slender below the ribs, and so ample about the pelvis. She curves outwards from the waist down, widening generously at the thighs, and then curving in again. Her bottom is the roundest, softest thing, with a deep cleft dividing it. Her pubic hair is soft and very long. Light dapples her body, just like in a Renoir.

I feel myself gloriously exposed to the sunlight. I glance down and watch my penis stir in its bush of wiry hairs. Inge watches this stirring also. She leans over and kisses my stomach. Then she curls herself around my lower half and begins coaxing me into full stiffness. The sun beams down on us. And later I raise her thigh and slide myself in underneath her. My large erection goes up her a long way.

She rolls her hips deliciously as I push into her wetness, then pull almost out of her, then push into her again. Inge's not on the pill or anything. Inge's not on the pill.

THE PHONE rang. It was Laura. 'Come to a party,' she said. Harry accepted.

It was some months after he had come back from Manila. Inge had gone off to do research in Egypt. He had not managed to trace Delphina. She had left no forwarding address. Perhaps she had gone back, behind the Iron Curtain. He had rung colleagues of hers at the Courtauld, but to no avail.

He had also called at Rosemary's flat. It turned out that she had left it some two months earlier, but the new tenant told him where she had gone to live. It was nearby. He walked to the new address.

Earlier it had been raining. A few drips still kept falling from the Spring leaves, and the wet streets gleamed where they curved away from their broken yellow lines. Night had just fallen, and the street-lamps had been lit. Nobody was about.

He found the house. It seemed very spacious, from the outside; and from the bells he guessed that it had been divided into three flats. Her name was on none of the bells. He tried pushing the top bell and was about to push the middle one when the door opened.

Rosemary stood there. He smiled his hello, but when she saw him her face became guarded. Even in the poor light from the street-lamps he could tell that she was pregnant. She made no move to let him in.

Instead she said, 'What do you want?'

'Just wondered how you were.' Harry began to feel awkward.

'I heard what happened. I don't want to see you again.'

'That's ok. I understand. I won't come in. How are things going?'

'Alright. As you can see, I managed it. It's his, the bloke upstairs. He's quite nice about it. We're living together now. I'm not fooling around anymore.'

'I suppose not. Oh well, it was nice seeing you again. Good luck, Rosemary.'

'Thanks.' She began to close the door.

'Goodbye,' he said, but the door had closed. He paused for a moment on the porch and then descended the steps. Thrusting his hands deep in his pockets, he walked to the nearest station. From there he caught the tube home.

It was as he came through the front door that the phone rang. The party was scheduled for Saturday night.

It was a good party. His hostess Laura seemed even larger than usual. Her huge breasts jostled inside the smock dress which came down to her ankles. When Harry arrived she embraced him. Harry cuddled her back. She felt truly massive. He handed her a bottle of wine, and she welcomed him loudly and began introducing him to people.

Laura had a very engaging smile and a warm manner. She always indulged her friends. Being fairly well off, and American by origin, she was able to throw parties where there was always lots to eat and where the booze flowed very freely indeed. Harry often came to her house for a smoke.

At that party, he drank steadily from the moment of his arrival. Just recently he had not been looking after himself well. His hair was unkempt, and there was stubble on his chin. He had not been to the launderette for a while, and he was suffering rather badly from Athlete's Foot.

Many of Laura's friends happened not to be artists. Most of them were cronies of hers from the local. By chance Dick was there, and other than Laura he was the only person Harry knew. But Dick cut Harry dead. There had been no real communication between them since the Rosemary business, though Dick remained Inge's friend, and had indeed been at the funeral. Harry kept at the drink. The talk was not about poetry or painting. People were full of the Russian gymnastics team which had just swept up most of the prizes at Munich.

'That Olga Korbut, how old is she anyway?'

'Seventeen, I think they said.'

'She doesn't look a day over twelve.'

'Isn't she fantastic? Did you watch her on the mat? I've never seen anything like it.'

Harry could not contain himself.

'I can do a flick-flack,' he cried.

'What's a flick-flack?' someone asked.

'It's a leap backwards. You sort of arch your body and then turn upside-down in the air to land on your hands and then on your feet. If you don't believe me, watch. Come on, clear a space.'

Soon a space was cleared for him by quite a few unimpressed people (including Dick, of course) drifting into another room. Harry kicked off his shoes and stood in the centre of the space. He pulled off his socks. Next, he lifted his arms, then brought them down to his sides as he bent his knees. Then up and over in the air he went, jumping, and arching his back with the jump, to land first on his hands and then again on his feet. Yes, it was a perfect flick-flack.

But everyone held their noses. Many more left the room. Harry had not changed his socks for weeks.

And now he burst into tears. Laura held him and took him into the bathroom. He sobbed and sobbed, dampening her smock at the front. The tears were like retching. He could not stop. They hurt him. And yet it was very good to cry. Laura pulled him against her bosom. A concerned guest looked in at him from the doorway. Laura helped him wash his feet. He still continued to sob. He was not in tears for the sake of the people watching.

INGE FELL ON the bed in the clothes she had worn for days. She did not bother to get under the bedclothes. I took off my trousers and got into bed properly. Despite the drums and the ululating women in the village square, Inge was soon fast asleep.

I found it more difficult to sleep, although I was utterly exhausted. I lay curled with my eyes closed and began dreaming before getting properly unconscious. I half-dreamt that I was still on a camel. Under my eyelids I could see the long, slow shadow of my carrier, or else the creature's neck and ears. We rode lurchingly onward across the unchanging desert. Every time I began falling asleep I felt that I was slipping off and falling towards the ground.

I would come wide awake with a start. Evening fell and deepened into night.

DAWN GIVES a sudden wail. It's hell changing her nappy.

THE NEXT MORNING tea was served in small glasses. Inge sat up. Daylight filtered in through the shutters. There was no sound from the village.

She went over to the small basin and washed her face. Harry sat up in the bed in his shirt and tie, sipping his tea. When he had finished it, he bent over and put the glass down on the sand-sprinkled floor.

Inge was using the towel on her face. She had slept all night in her clothes.

'Come back to bed,' Harry grunted. 'And take your clothes off too.'

'I don't want to,' Inge replied through the towel.

Harry jumped out of bed and grabbed her by the arms. He threw her on the bed and pushed her down.

'Even if you don't, I'm going to bloody make you.'

Inge struggled hard to get from underneath him.

Harry shook her violently.

'You'll bloody do what *I* want.'

He sat on her chest, and despite her arching her back she really could not dislodge him. He tugged off his tie with one hand and used it to fasten her wrists together. Then he snatched up a scarf that lay on the bed and used that to fasten her wrists to the iron rail at its head.

'Get off me, Harry,' she gasped in exasperation, still trying to twist away.

Naked but for his shirt, he got off her and went to the suitcase. She could not unfasten her wrists.

Finding another scarf and another tie, he came back to the bed. Then he unzipped her slacks and yanked them off her. Next he tugged down her panties, and soon he had secured her ankles to the foot of the bed. He straddled her again and unbuttoned her shirt. Finally he reached underneath her, and after fumbling for a while he succeeded in unfastening her brassiere.

Now she lay tightly bound; her breasts bare, her thighs exposed and spread.

'Let me get up now.'

'Not on your life.'

He pushed his knuckles into her. She was wet. This made him hard. He rubbed the hard part of himself along the groove beneath her pubic hair. Again and again he did this. She tried to squeeze her thighs together, then she tried to roll away. Harry held her apart and bent and sucked her. Just for a moment he raised his head.

'I am going to rape your cunt,' he said.

Again she tried to close her knees. Again he forced them apart. He pushed against her and slid into her. He moved in and out.

Then he stopped. He lay still.

And then he took it out. He reached for his pants and pulled them on.

'Why did you stop? Why did you stop?'

'WHAT ABOUT NOW then?'

'Now? You want to go to a fight right now? Very well. Come on, Jun. Let's take Harry to a fight.'

But what comes out of that visit to the cockfight is the lovely head of the Infant; the child Jesus which looks so like a girl, with the one jewel remaining attached to an ear. Battered forehead, scraped nose, and her single eye so bright. It's that, and the inclination of her head, and the sheer delicacy of her temples. Well, it's easy to say of a work of art, that is so alive. But the actuality of the living-ness in this tiny ikon is something quite particular. It touches me in the pit of my stomach. It's the one sign.

I buy it. I purchase her. Words like buy or purchase seem an insult.

I may be buying an object in Manila – but more deeply I'm sanctifying a presence in my heart. Money is passed over the counter, sure it is. But that's not the point. The brown shop keeper wraps up the Infant and hands the purchase to me.

Entering the hotel is like walking into an ice-box.

WHEN I GOT back to my hotel-room in Manila, I found a girl waiting for me there. She was very slim and brown and pretty, but she had a large wart-like growth on the end of her nose. She held her finger to her lips and swiftly closed the door behind me.

'They must not know I am here,' she said.

I wondered how she had managed to slip past the policeman at the end of the corridor.

'I must not be found here,' she explained in a whisper.

'If they find me they will put me in prison.'

'Why did you come? It's dangerous. You will get us both into trouble.'

'I had to come. You are an observer-delegate. I have come to tell you that things are not as they wish you to see them. People are put into prison.'

'I know that. You did not have to come to tell me this. I have Philippine friends in London. Many have told me how things are here.'

'The leader of our opposition is in prison. And there is the curfew. When you get home you must write about conditions here. There is no freedom.'

'I know about this. You must keep your voice down. There is a policeman at the end of the corridor.'

'He did not see me come up here. He went for a piss, the pig. I slipped in when this corridor was empty. It is my duty to tell you of these things.'

'Do you like to fuck? The pretty girls who look after me at the congress, they like to smile and stroke my arms. They never want to fuck.'

'Yes, I sometimes like to fuck, but now I want to tell you of our brothers and our sisters in the prisons here. Conditions, conditions are bad.'

'I cannot help,' I said, putting my arm around her. 'I am only a visitor here, a guest. I have no power to help at all.' My hand squeezed her bottom. It was soft. I pushed her back against the bed, thrusting my tongue in her mouth. Then I unzipped my trousers.

'I have not come to fuck,' she said. 'I have come to tell you of conditions in the slums. Have you seen? Behind the high, white wall? Please, I do not wish to fuck. I want for you to understand conditions here.'

I had taken my clothes off. My penis stuck out hard against her dress.

'You must not speak too loud,' I said.

'I know, they must not find me here. Oh, please be careful now. I do not really want.'

We both spoke in whispers all the time. I lifted her dress and pushed it up over her breasts. I slid a hand across her brown stomach.

'Now I want to fuck,' I said.

She squeezed her legs together, but not with enough strength to stop me removing her panties. I raised her bare brown legs and tried to forget the wart on her nose. I moistened her vagina.

'I do not really want to do this.'

'I want to do it,' I said.

'Ah, but you know I must not be found. Please be careful. Do not make a noise.'

I held her firm and pushed it in.

'Ow, it is hurting,' she whispered. 'Stop.'

I waited. Then I pushed it further in.

'It hurts,' she said. 'It hurts.'

Soon I pulled it out, and my sperm went shooting over her brown belly.

Then I got up and gave her a towel. I put on my pants and trousers. She put on her panties and then pulled down her dress.

'Now you'd better go,' I said. 'Let me take a look. If the coast is clear, you should be able to get away.'

I opened the door and looked out. The corridor was empty. I motioned with my head. She slipped past and was gone.

I sat down on the bed.

About the Author

Anthony Howell is a poet and novelist whose first collection, *Inside the Castle* was brought out in 1969. He was invited to the International Writers Program, University of Iowa in 1971. *His Analysis of Performance Art* is published by Routledge. In 1997 he was short-listed for a Paul Hamlyn Award. *Plague Lands*, his versions of Iraqi poet Fawzi Karim, was a 2011 Poetry Book Society Recommendation. *The Step is the Foot* – his analysis of the relationship of dance to poetry – is published by Grey Suit Editions. *Incomprehensible Lesson* – his second book of Karim's poems – was shortlisted for the Sarah Maguire Prize 2021. He is a Hawthornden fellow and has recorded poems for The Poetry Archive. The author's first novel, *In the Company of Others* (Marion Boyars, 1983), set in a ballet company, was greeted with praise for the flair with which the author captured the world of dance. In it, as Jonathan Keates wrote in the *Observer*, "the strident, coarse actualities of its sanctified self-absorption are brought monstrously to life."

Other books by Grey Suit Editions

Donald Gardner
New and Selected Poems 1966–2020
£14.95

Anthony Howell
The Step is the Foot
Dance and its relationship to poetry
£14.99

Gwendolyn Leick
Gertrude Mabel May
An ABC of Gertrude Stein's Love Triangle
£14.99

Walter Owen
The Cross of Carl
AN ALLEGORY
Preface by General Sir Ian Hamilton
£9.95

Iliassa Sequin
Collected Complete Poems
£14.95

*We also publish chapbooks by Donald Gardner, Alan Jenkins,
Fawzi Karim, Lorraine Mariner, Kerry-Lee Powell, Pamela
Stewart, Rosanne Wasserman and Hugo Williams*